A TROPICAL FRONTIER

A Tropical Frontier, by Tim Robinson

Pioneers and Settlers of Southeast Florida
(A comprehensive history)

Tales of Old Florida

The Homesteaders

The Gladesman

The Cow Hunters

Time Rummers:
Or, How Gnarles and Paddy Saved the Day

The Hermit

The Good Dog

The Indian Fighter

The River

A Salty Tale

The Legacy

The Last Caloosa

The Deep Blue Sea

The Brigand

The Outpost

The Reef

Milton's Big Night Out

The Quest

The Curse of Jamba Lona

The Good Mother

GONE WITH THE WOOF

A Bad Dog Book

TIM ROBINSON

Port Sun Publishing
PORT SALERNO, FLORIDA

ISBN: 9798401140852

Printed and bound in the USA.

Cover design, Patrick Robinson

To Buddy-boy

Gone with the Woof

(Based on true events)

Prologue

"Buuuuuuuddy!"

Did I hear something?

"Here, Buddy Boy! Come on, Buddy!"

I know that rabbit's around here somewhere. Sniff, sniff.

"Buddy! Come on! Let's go!"

Oh, yeah. Someone's calling; sounds like Aunt Charlotte. But I just know that rascally rabbit is hidin' around here somewhere.

"BUDDY!! BAD DOG!! COME!!"

Oo. Bad dog, huh? All right, fine.

With that, the big, brown dog gave up the trail and headed back home at a casual trot.

"BUDDY!! BAD DOG!!"

I'm comin'. I'm comin'. Keep your pants on.

He was almost there. The green barn was coming into view, the house was beyond it. Aunt Charlotte was on the porch, hands on hips, dishtowel in hand, and a frown on her face. Almost there.

Wait a minute. What's that? A new smell? I'd better investigate.

And off Buddy went, into the orange grove.

Chapter One

This was war.

It wasn't one of these minor cat-chasing-mouse things you hear about. It wasn't even lion-chasing-antelope or man-hunting-lion, a struggle in which one party has a distinct advantage over the other. No, this was war. Real war. It was a contest of equals: the top players in the animal kingdom vying one against the other for ultimate supremacy.

Yes, this was war. Real war.

This was Man (and Buddy) versus Armadillo.

Pappy and Buddy stared with consternation down the hole under the porch.

Pap pushed his straw hat back on his bald head. He scratched contemplatively at his beard. He set his hands firmly on his hips.

Both combatants wore deep, furrowed, contemplative scowls. As to their faces, the one was quite handsome behind the freight of hard-won years and a long, gray beard; the other was handsome as well, with engaging brown eyes and a wide, black, attractive muzzle. He wore a naturally philosophical expression.

"Dag-nabbed armadillies."

Yeah. Dag-nabbed armadillies, Buddy, the big brown dog, agreed.

Of course, if there were no rules to war, it would be a *fait accompli*. Pappy would have, by now, gone for Old Hildegard and scattered a load of yeehaw off the offensive intruder's hard, buckshot-proof hide. Yes, it would be done and over by now. At the very least, they would have sent him, or her, packing, down the grassy lane, never to return. But there were rules to war these days, and the no-shooting rule had been ratified and enacted some time ago by Grandma. It was the day, in fact, that she had seen a mommy armadillo with her three adorable baby armadillos trailing along behind.

"But," Pappy had resisted, "what if it's a male armadilly? Can I shoot it then? Birdshot only?"

The edict had been a resounding, "Not likely, buster."

Pappy and Buddy were wondering exactly what they were dealing with here. Buddy thought it was a male.

"Are you sure?" Pappy asked.

Not at all, Buddy replied in his way.

"Maybe you should just go down there and bring it out," Pappy suggested. "You are the farm dog, you know."

Uh ... no thanks, Buddy replied. *Didn't I hear you telling Grandma that armadillos have leprosy?*

"Well," Pappy hemmed. "I didn't say they *have* leprosy. I said they are *known to carry* leprosy."

Well, I don't want to take a chance on that, getting leprosy ... whatever that is. Buddy scratched his big head. *What is leprosy, anyway?*

Pappy scratched his long, gray beard. "I'm not sure, really. But you're probably right. You don't want ta be takin' a chance on it."

Exactly, Buddy agreed. *Anyway, I've already tried picking one up, remember? They just roll into a ball and I can't get my mouth around it.*

Pappy studied Buddy's mouth.

"It's not a real long mouth, is it, Budiford? Not a lot of grasping room there."

Don't reckon so, Buddy replied.

Once again, Man and Dog stared down the hole.

"Well," Pappy said, "desperate times call for desperate measures."

Yep, Buddy agreed. *So, what you got in mind?*

"Only the most desperate of measures, my old pal Budiford. I'm gonna put out some money, that's what."

Buddy's engaging, brown eyes displayed surprise. Shock even.

Really?

"That's right. Really. You and me, we're goin' ta town right now, down ta Cousin Travis's, and get us a varmint trap. It's not like I'm bein' impulsive; I've always wanted one. Might use it ta catch us some 'a those durn-testable raccoons that keep comin' 'round here, causin' all kinds 'a grief for me ... and you."

Durn-testable raccoons, Buddy concurred.

With that, Pappy yelled into the house through the open Dutch door, "Me and Buddy's goin' ta town!"

"All right!" Several voices shouted back from the kitchen. Then, "Oh wait, Pap!"

It was Grandma.

"Could you get these few things down at Uncle Moe's?"

Pappy and Buddy looked at each other, sighed, and turned around for the list.

Buddy waited while Pappy got his list, and his kiss. Then they were off.

A minute later, they were in Big Red, Pappy's cranky, old, pick-up truck, driving down the grassy lane. They passed Star, the giant, useless but beautiful and graceful racehorse, and Okee Donkey – none of those things.

Buddy stuck his head out the window and shouted *adios:*

"Woof!"

5

*   *   *

Buddy was in his prime; maybe not even *to* his prime yet.

It's good to be a dog.

It was a normal day on patrol, early shift. He had seen Pap off to work, the kids off to school, and now it was time to go to work himself.

On patrol.

The first stop, of course, was to check on that dastardly armadillo under the back porch. Buddy hated sharing his under-the-porch with an armadillo. The thought of leprosy cooties sent an icy shiver up his spine. He had barked at it, growled, snarled, and even bared his teeth, but armadillos were apparently fearless – or really stupid.

He said his hellos to Star and Oke, then proceeded towards the chicken coop and barn.

Sniff, sniff. It was the name of the game.

Of course, the raccoons had been here overnight, as always. *Durn-testable raccoons.* All had looked secure, however, upon his first inspection this morning, at sunrise. On the farm, everyone got up with the sun – everyone except Cock-a-doodle-done-did.

Done-did, as he was commonly called, was just now getting up and around.

Pappy said he was gonna eat Cock-a-doodle-done-did one of these days if he didn't start getting up before lunchtime.

"Beer-neese sauce!" Pappy would declare. "I'll smother him in Beer-neese sauce!"

The big rooster yawned, cock-suredly, and scratched an itch.

"Have a good morning?" Buddy asked Cock-a-doodle-done-did.

"Not bad, suh," the rooster replied.

Cock-a-doodle-done-did was from the south, of Rhode Island. He spoke with a long, cool drawl, which was known to drive the young hens wild with feathery, swoonful desire.

"I do, I say I do declare that those rascally raccoons attempted to gain entry into the coop again, as you can plainly see."

"Hm," Buddy said, inspecting the bent wire and the clawed ground in front of the coop door. "I don't think they can get in. Pappy put a board there on the bottom. See?"

"I do see, suh; but that is not the point. These poor, defenseless ladies, who depend on you and others for security, are in a dither!"

"A ... dither?" Buddy said.

"Yes! Dither. In fact, they are bein' terrorized. Terrorized, I say! Why, it is a disgrace that you and your Pappy have done absolutely nothin' to assuage this problem. Why, sometimes these young damsels, who are in my charge, are traumatized to the point that, well, let's just say theah's a reason for my presence heah, and it is not only to look good, even though I do." He paused. "Rhode Island Red, ya know."

"Uh, yeah," Buddy replied. "I do know. And what is it you want me to do about it?"

"Why, I wish for you to speak to your Pappy about it. Express ta him the dire nature of this predicament. Why, I would not be surprised if this is havin' a deleterious effect on egg pro-duction."

"Really?" Buddy asked.

"Oh, absolutely. Why, what we really need around heah is twenty-four hour security."

"Twenty-four hour security? What are you talkin' about?"

Cock-a-doodle-done-did shook his head disparagingly, and said, "We need you, or someone like you, a big, strong fightin' machine, to be on duty twenty-four hours a day. There are terrors and threats aplenty, all around us!" he drawled, sweeping his wing in a broad arc.

"I gotta tell you," Buddy replied. "That's not gonna happen. Grandma wants me in every night. She thinks I'll get hurt out here, or get lost or something."

"Has she no confidence in you, suh?"

"Oh, she has confidence. She just worries a lot."

"Well, it seems ta me that the most important time for you ta be out here is at night!"

"I can't argue with you, Done-did. But that's a steep hill to climb in that house. And I gotta tell you, it is nice and cozy in there at night."

"I imagine it is," Done-did replied with a wistful sigh.

Dog and rooster looked to the big, rambling, two-story farm house in the orange grove.

"Well, if you could just mention it to your Pappy, it would be kindly appreciated, suh."

"I'll mention it to him," Buddy said, "but that's all I can do."

Buddy continued on: *sniff, sniff.*

Pee.

He loped on past the barn and the barn apartment that Uncle Amos lived in, then past the barnyard, where Grandma had a flower garden by the big oak tree, then down the fence-line towards the lake. He picked up the scent of fox. Yes, a fox had been to the coop last night as well. Buddy had not seen the point of informing Cock-a-doodle-done-did of that tidbit.

"Darned fox," Buddy mumbled under his breath.

A minute later, he was to the lake. He waded in, up to his belly. He drank up. Buddy thought lake water was the best tasting water, even though Pappy had told him drinking lake water would give him gills. Buddy did not think having gills would be such a bad thing, though.

Out of the water. A big, tumultuous shake. Up the grassy bank for a good, woofy roll.

Ahh. Oo. Ahh.

It's good to be a dog.

He got up and shook. He looked around, then across the lake to the stand of cypress there on the southwest shore. Beyond that, he could catch glimpses of the far fence-line. His eyes scanned the area, searching for any sign of intruders, very specifically, canine intruders.

All clear. He proceeded back to the grassy lane and along there all the way to the gate by the County Road. He sniffed the air, and a few more things. Then he turned south, making his way in an investigative manner along the fence-line, searching out any sign of unauthorized incursion. To his right were the pine and palmetto woods and beyond that, Pappy's lemon grove – his pride and joy, or so he would declare: "A sour grove for a sour puss!"

Buddy was making his way along a stretch of saw palmetto. All of a sudden, he stopped. He sniffed at the ground. He looked around.

"Shawn O'Shady," he mumbled under his breath. "Oh, he was definitely snooping around here last night. Maybe old Done-did is onto something. It might be a good thing if I were on patrol, or at least available, over the nighttime hours." Buddy's eyes grew pointed. "How many times have I told that fox?"

He sniffed around a little more. His extra broad brow furrowed deeply. He cocked his head one way, then the other.

Do I hear snoring? Hm.

He stuck his nose deeper into the saw palmetto.

"Dag-nabbit!" Then, "Hey. Hey! Wake up!"

"Huh?" the sleeping form grunted. "What?"

Green eyes opened slowly. Then they noticed the giant head sticking under the fronds and popped three times wide.

Without moving a muscle, as if frozen in place, Shawn O'Shady looked one way, then the other, and said, "Oh, hey. Uh … um, how ar-r-re ya, me lovely?"

Buddy scowled. "I'm not your lovely, O'Shady. And you know full well that you're on the wrong side of that fence-line. How many times have I told you to stay off this side of the fence-line? Otherwise, I'm gonna have to teach you a lesson."

Shawn O'Shady shrugged sheepishly, and said, "Ah, me good dog, 'tis ooonly a short way from the fence-line, it is. And I was tired last night, after a long night 'o huntin' and for-r-ragin'."

"Foraging around my chicken coop," Buddy grumbled.

8

Shawn shrugged again, sheepishly, and said, "Ohh, t'was just seein' how me old fr-r-riends was gettin' along is all. Why, I'd never try anything here, at your place. No, 'tis too well fortified, it is. I just stop by for, for nostalgic reasons is all. It takes me back to a time before ya ever come along – and before your Pappy fortified the coop, might I add."

"Yeah. Well, I don't want you coming around anymore, hear? And no more staying over when you do … not that you're gonna be."

Shawn O'Shady stretched. He yawned.

"Fine," he sighed. "But 'tis such a nice stoppin' over place, it is. So much pleasanter than across the r-r-roooad or on the other side of the fence-line. Here, I knooow I won't be accosted by those rascally and ill-natured Sinister Six."

"Oh, great," Buddy said, setting his paws on his hips. "And what am I? Chopped liver? You don't think I can tear you limb from limb?"

"Ohh, I suppooose ya might, but 'tis wiser ta take me chances with you, laddie. We've all heard about the 'baby r-r-rabbit' incident, ya knooow. When ya was still a lop-footed pup? Word gets around when it comes ta such things. They say ya was despondent for weeks. Wouldn't eat your kibble, they say. Stayed up late at night and howled forlornly at the moooon. 'Tis not that I'm not afraid of ya. I most certainly am. Why just look at those broad shoooulders and that trim waistline. I certainly dun'na wish ta be on your bad side. Nooo, I dooon't. We've all heard what ya did ta Bob Cat that time she got all pushy because ya was just a pup still, and she makin' fun 'a your giant, bulbous head. But," Shawn O'Shady shrugged, "I was still a long way from me hooome last night, and I was in need of a place ta r-r-rest me fine Ir-r-rish head."

Buddy scowled. He wasn't that crazy about long talkers. He had to get back to work.

"All right," he mumbled. "Just don't make it a habit, all right? I got a reputation to maintain. You know?"

"'Tis not a problem, me good dog. Ya won't be a'troubled by the likes 'a me again."

With that, Shawn O'Shady got to his feet, nodded, and dashed through the fence, out to the road. Without looking, he sprinted across – just as a car was passing!

"Look out!" Buddy shouted, but it was too late, and the car went right over him.

Then it was gone, and there was Shawn O'Shady on the other side, a wide grin on his red Irish face.

"'Tis the luck 'a the Ir-r-rish, it is!" he shouted, and off he bounded with his bushy red tail, into the woods.

Buddy watched a while. Then he shook his head, and mumbled, "Foxes. Sheesh."

A while later, he got to the end of the fence, turned west, and headed down the fence-line, towards the cypress head and Icky Springs.

Shawn was right. He was a pushover. A real softie.

Buddy recalled the time he cornered a rabbit out by the barn.

The rabbit had cowered against the wall like John Dillinger in the headlights.

"What," the rabbit had stammered in fear, "what're ya gonna do to me?"

Buddy had looked around, and mumbled, "Uhh … nothin'. Go on. Get out 'a here."

It can be tough for a dog to live some things down.

The scent of dog, unauthorized dog, grated on Buddy more than any other. Why, it was worse than foxes, cats, raccoons, or any other denizens of the forest for that matter.

The south fence-line was the boundary between The Last Resort, which was Pappy's place, and Old Man Perkins's place, which was known along the prairie and even around town as "The Grunge." It was so-named because of all the old cars, boats, trailers, and farm equipment parked out front.

Old Man Perkins had never sold any of them. They just sat out there and rotted.

Folks from out of town, city folk, would sometimes stop by and let themselves onto the property to look them over. Sometimes they'd even head on up to the house. A few minutes later, there they'd come, racing down the drive with a pack of wild, uncouth dogs right on their heels, squealing their tires when they hit the pavement of the County Road. Sometimes a shotgun blast or two could be heard just before the revving engine, barking dogs, and squealing tires.

It would be amusing if it weren't so disturbing – especially if you were the neighbor; and more especially if you were the one in charge of security; and most especially if you were Buddy.

It was the only thing bad about the 240 acres, those mean, old, grungy neighbors next door, from Old Man Perkins all the way down to Viper, the miniature shih tzu, who never stopped yapping twenty-four hours a day.

Oh, how Buddy loathed those neighbor dogs. Folks all along the prairie, and even in town, referred to them as the Sinister Six. As far as Buddy was concerned, it was a fitting name. It used to be the Fiendish Five, but then the one-legged chihuahua showed up a while back, so now it was the Sinister Six.

That is one scary ankle-chomper, that chihuahua.

Pappy had to reinforce the fence along this section several years ago, just to keep them from getting in and terrorizing Grandma's chickens. Oh, they were bad dogs; bad, bad dogs. There was no doubt about that.

Buddy loped along the lakeshore, sniffing here, peeing there, performing his sworn duties.

Oh, does it stink over here! Mm, mm, mm.

Yes, that was the problem with the south fence-line: the smell of dog, unauthorized dog. Sinister dog.

The fence-line passed right through Icky Springs, which was just a low, swampy depression that flowed, during high water, into the cypress head and then the lake. It had not been an actual flowing spring since Mr. Disston had shown up years ago with the intent of draining all the water out of Florida. He didn't finish the job, but there were other men who had – job well done. Even then, from what Buddy had heard, it had never been a very productive, or appealing, stream of water, even back in the old days.

Buddy's ears perked. His broad brow furrowed.

He frantically sniffed at the ground. His hackles reared. The hairs stood rigid on the back of his neck.

With his nose to the ground, he followed the trail, right to Icky Springs.

Darn it! Those dad-blasted neighbor dogs have been over here!

Buddy was beside himself.

He scoured the ground, looking for pawprints. All he could find were two sets: the chihuahua's, which were easy to spot because it only had three legs, and –

Viper! That little, loud, yappy one!

Buddy's blood boiled as he continued his investigation, creeping along the muddy, mucky edges of the spring, along the cattails, over to the fence-line.

Closely, he inspected it.

Oh, no! The fence! It's been compromised!

Yes, there was a tiny hole at the bottom, big enough only for Viper to get through. But Buddy could see they had been excavating around it. There were pawprints of many sizes, where they had tried to gain entry.

Buddy was collecting more evidence when he heard it: that old, familiar, irritating sound of wild, unruly dogs charging in his direction. He sighed and backed up a step or two. He braced himself. He watched as the dogs, led by the big Doberman Pinscher, bounded across the field and rushed right up to the fence, barking insanely, growling, and baring their teeth.

My gosh, that little one is annoying.

Speaking of which, the little one, Viper, without a moment's hesitation, went right for the hole in the fence.

Also without hesitation, Buddy lunged. Viper changed her mind and was back through the hole.

"You'd better tell that little poop-tzu, or whatever she is, to stay on your side of the line," Buddy warned, speaking to all of them but looking at Ivanovic, or Vic, the big Doberman Pinscher.

"Hmph," Vic snorted, glancing at Viper. "Do not worry about her, *Herr* Fat Head."

11

"It's *Big* Head, your Doofiness. And Pappy says big heads hold more brains than little ones. From the looks of it, you got a peanut up there."

Buddy was aware that Vic was self-conscious about his, as Pappy would say, "innate lack of calculability and figure-it-outiveness."

Buddy felt an inner glow. There was nothing more satisfying, in his mind, than getting under Vic's skin. He didn't really do it on purpose – or at least that wasn't how it had started when he arrived for duty here. It was just so much fun, though; and it was so, so easy.

Vic got all uptight, like he did. His upper lip curled way up on the front, so that his mouth looked like an exaggerated clown's, or like he had tried to eat a horseshoe and it got stuck.

The other dogs looked on as Vic tried to find his thoughts – or thought. His face looked as if it might pop and launch that peanut-sized brain like a rocket ship to the moon.

"Look! Fat Head!" he said in a heavy German accent. "Ve know zhat cat of yours –"

Buddy calmly interrupted, raising his paw.

"I gotta tell you, she's not mine. She's not anyone's. Grandma happens to feed her, and she does live in the house; but she comes and goes as she pleases. According to Pappy, she belongs to no one."

Vic looked momentarily flummoxed. No, it wasn't momentary. He glared at Buddy and snarled, like a clown with a horseshoe in his mouth, and stammered, "Vhat … stop interrupting me! Vhat … whoefer's cat it is –"

"She's no one's."

"I … mph … I … don't care! Zhat … zhat CAT has been coming ofer here and prowling around at night! Leafing cat smell all over zhe place. Here! Zhere! Eferyvhere!! I just … I just … " it looked like that peanut might come flying out, "I just cannot stand it! Zhere is nozhing more disgusting zhan cat poop!!"

Buddy shrugged. "You ever seen ferret poop?"

"Huh? Vhat? Vhat are you … a … a ferret? Vhat zhe heck is a ferret? I mean … Stop interrupting me!"

"Oh. Sorry. Go ahead. You were talking about cat poop."

"*Ya'vol!*" Vic snarled. "I hate cat poop!"

"But don't you have cats over there? I know you have cats over there because they come over here all the time. Do I complain to you about that? No. I know how it is with cats. They have no respect for boundaries." Buddy paused. "You know something about boundaries, don't you, Vic? Respecting boundaries? Or … *not* respecting them?"

Buddy could see Vic was having trouble with that one, enough that Lionel, the beagle, spoke up.

"He's sayin' that you don't respect boundaries either, Vic."

Even with that, it took a minute to sink in.

Then, finally, "You ... You ... You are saying zhat I am like a ... a cat?!"

"You said that, Vic," Buddy mumbled. "I just said some folks have problems with understanding boundaries, like cats. And you."

The air erupted in rage and bristle as Vic rushed the fence, ramming his narrow, angular head through one of the holes and shaking the entire section of fence. His teeth – a really good set by the way – were bared and threatening. Behind him were the others, barking madly, howling, and using inappropriate, insulting language, calling Buddy all kinds of names – names much worse than Fat Head, by the way.

Buddy, meanwhile, sighed and watched the gauche display of unruly displeasure.

He figured he ought to do something, so he ran up and down the fence-line and barked, warning them to stay on their side – or else.

This went on a while.

Then the boxer, Ali, instead of hurling insults at Buddy, barked, "Hey! It's Old Man Perkins! He's calling us!"

It took a few times because six dogs, seven if you count Buddy, can make a lot of racket.

The barking tapered off, and Cornwall, the overweight English hound, took off for home, followed soon after by the others. Vic gave Buddy a final snarl and sneer and ran off as well, leaving only Buddy and Lionel, the beagle.

They snarled at each other.

"You better get goin'," Buddy said. "I hear Old Man Perkins is a crotchety old son of Beelzebub."

"You should watch your mouth, Big Head. He's our master, you know."

"Master," Buddy chuckled.

"What's so funny?"

"Here, at my place, The Last Resort, there is no master – or implied slave. We're all friends here. We're all pals."

"Hmph," Lionel snorted. "Have they got you fooled. Do they tell you to do tricks, like sit, stay, lie down, roll over, and beg? Oh, that's a good one, begging."

Buddy scowled.

"Sure," he said. "I do a few of those things. Sometimes that's just what I need to do, sit or lie down. And Davy has me do some of those other things, sure. He's my boy, and I like making my boy happy, so I do it." He paused. "Actually, I do pretty well with the begging on my own."

"That's a good one," Lionel chuckled. "But I'm telling you, you need to keep that cat out of here. We gotta put up with our own cats. We don't need any more around here."

"Oh. And you're gonna keep your cats off my property?"

Lionel's eyes narrowed. He glanced down the trail through the woods to home.

"Look," he said. "I'm just warning you, understand? Vic can be a little vindictive. Get it? Vindictive Vic? You'd best listen to me, Mr. Big Pants. Those others do whatever he says to do." He paused, then added, "You'd best take heed, mister."

With that, Lionel, the beagle, turned and hurried towards home.

Buddy scowled. It was a dire warning.

Chapter Two

Outside, in the middle of the day, it was a weekday on the farm. It wasn't *always* the same old thing. If you weren't looking closely, however, it might appear so.

Marvin had a bird's eye view from up on the telephone pole. As far as he could see, this was his domain. And Mabel's. Marv and Mabel Mockingbird, they were.

Nobody messed with the mockingbirds. If they did, they knew what they would get.

Actually, Marvin left the dirty work to Mabel. She had the appropriate disposition for such things, especially when there were young'ns involved. She was over on the barn roof now, keeping watch, or rather making sure Marv was keeping watch – and that he was singing.

He mumbled under his breath, "I don't know what she's so worried about. Our nest is in the bougainvillea bush. No one's stupid enough to go in there after the kids."

And singing!

Marv saw Mabel looking his way. He sighed.

"She always wants something new and original," he mumbled, and he started in with a lively – but bluesy – number.

It was indeed a fine view, though it was the same goings on as usual, mostly: one thing and another.

The cat, that big black and white one, was standing at the gate between the house and the old wash house, which was small. Nowadays, it was used as a playhouse, fort, ship at sea, or whatever.

Regardless, as usual, the dog was staring at the cat, right on the other side of the little, picket gate. He stared a while – as usual – then he all of a sudden dashed around the tiny wash house to get to the cat on the other side. Alas, every time the dog got there – every time – the cat had already stepped through the slat to the other side.

At the moment, the dog was on this side; the cat was on the other.

Riveting action.

Marv was singing his heart out, letting the world know he was watching over his nest – and mighty happy to do it, too.

He noticed the back door to the house open and heard the familiar whoosh of a broom. Old broom bristles were some of the best nest-making materials known to bird-dom. He watched a minute. Then the woman came out and looked around the corner, towards the birdfeeder, which the Mockingbird family did *not* partake of, by the way. Dining on dry, bland seeds was not exactly their idea of living it up, which is what mockingbirds do, obviously, by their constant and never-ending, joyous outbursts of song.

As expected, the woman charged around the corner and started swinging the broom and yelling at the squirrels to get away from the birdfeeder. One of them, she chased all the way out into the yard, past the old oak tree, almost all the way to the grassy lane.

Marv shook his head. He glanced at his wife and picked up his tempo.

The little girl came out to watch. On their way back inside, the woman paused, as always, to do a few last sweeps across the porch decking.

"Oo. Fresh nest-makings. Maybe I'll treat Mabel to a few tonight. Ba-ba-boom."

*   *   *

Grandmas are most often the one in charge, as it should be. It has probably been thus for many thousands of years, she being the axis upon which all other life swirls and perpetuates.

It was no different in this particular case. Everyone knew it. They knew this not by some dictate or fiat, but by natural instinct. Yes, it was instinctual not to tick off the person in charge of feeding them, clothing them, nurturing them, encouraging them, and of course, giving them life.

Grandma had a good handle on things; yes, she did.

Except for the squirrels.

"What is wrong with those things?!" she demanded, as usual, as she stormed back into the house after chasing them away. "I give them their own feed over by the oak tree, for goodness sake!"

She leaned the broom in the corner.

"That's not good for the bristles," the little girl, Annie, five going on thirty-five, noted.

Grandma sighed. "I know. But I'll be picking it up again in five minutes."

She looked out the kitchen window and sighed. She started looking around the window sill and casement, searching for something.

"I don't see him again this morning."

Gingerly, she pushed back some leaves on her window plant, looking for sign of movement.

"Davy says it's a gecko," Annie noted. "It sleeps during the day."

"Yes," Grandma said, delicately rummaging around, searching for signs of life.

"Pappy says you'll scare it away if you keep doing that. Pappy says –"

"I know what Pappy says," Grandma mumbled, giving up her search. She picked up a Big Red bottle cap, rinsed it out, and filled it. She took a moment to look out at the birdfeeder. It was still clear of squirrels. A cardinal, bunting, and a woodpecker were feeding in peace. But she could see them out there, staring back at her with those baleful, beady, squirrel eyes.

"Pappy also says you shouldn't feed the squirrels out by the oak tree because it just attracts more squirrels."

"Well, Pappy says a lot of things."

"Yep," Annie replied. "Davy says he's the smartest man in the world."

"I … he's … pretty smart," Grandma replied. Then she mumbled under her breath. "I suppose."

"What?"

"Nothing."

"Do you think Davy is on his field trip now?" Annie asked.

"Well, they were supposed to leave by ten-thirty." Grandma paused from her grandmotherly, kitchen-type duties and looked to the clock over the doorway leading to the dining room. "So, what time is it now?" she asked.

Annie looked at the clock, the big hand, and the little hand, and stammered, "It's … eleven?" She looked to Grandma, who gave her an encouraging nod. "Eleven … twenty?" A look and nod. "Eleven twenty … six."

"Very good. And is that after or before ten-thirty?"

Annie studied the clock. "After."

"That's right. So he should be with the other kids at the waste treatment plant right now."

"That's where all the poop goes!" Annie declared.

"Well, for the town people it is. Out here we, well, we have a septic tank, so we keep our poop right here, where we make it, as your Pappy might say. My Lord," Grandma sighed. "I think I'm turning into him."

"Well, I hope you don't grow a long beard like him," Annie giggled.

"Don't worry, sweetheart. If I notice whiskers starting to pop out on my face, I'll start shaving right away. You'll never even know it, unless I get five-o'clock shadow." She sighed. "My Lord, I am turning into him."

The two conspirators snickered with unfettered, multi-generational glee.

Mid-morning to mid-afternoon, it was usually just Grandma and Annie – and Buddy, Kitty, Star, and, of course, Okee Donkey.

HEEEEEE-HAWWWW!!

"I think Oke's getting hungry for his midday snack," Annie said, getting down from her kitchen chair. She got on her toes and peered out the open Dutch door, towards the turnout.

"Go ahead and get a carrot and some of that romaine leaf I set aside. We'll be going out in a minute." Grandma looked at the clock. "Where does the time go?"

A minute later, they were on the back porch, heading out to the barn.

"Why are you leaving the screen door cracked?" Annie asked.

"Just for a few minutes. It's for the gecko. I'm worried he doesn't have enough flies to eat in here."

"Oh," Annie replied. Then she took a deep breath, and shouted, "BUUUUUD-DYYYY!!"

A second later, the big, brown dog dashed around the corner of the playhouse. Joyous, doggy delight was splashed across his broad, heavy brow.

"Woof!"

*　　　*　　　*

"You sure these taste good?"

"Carrots? Delicious."

Buddy, Oke, and Star were munching on carrot bits. Buddy was sitting for his.

"How come you guys don't sit?"

Oke shook his head. "It's not a real good look for us."

"Oh."

Annie was doling out the treats judiciously, as instructed by Grandma, who was sweeping the barn for the third time that day.

Buddy didn't really get it. Dirt was good stuff. There were spots bare of grass all over the property where Buddy would lay and daydream, right there in the dirt. If Buddy heard it once, he'd heard it a thousand times: "Don't roll in that dirt, Buddy!" Mostly, it came from Grandma, but sometimes from Aunt Charlotte as well, and pretty much any woman in sight.

Buddy didn't understand women.

He understood men pretty well, he thought, and boys. They didn't seem to mind dirt so much, kind of like him. And Pappy. Buddy had seen Pap so filthy that even he had cringed.

It was usually just them, Buddy, Grandma, and Annie. Sometimes, though, on the weekends, holidays, summertime, or during Christmas or spring break, there could be as many as a dozen or more, kids caravanning out to join in with the barn chores. These chores were performed a minimum of five times per day: clean the stalls, fill the water, give treats or feed, check barn garden (water or weed if needed), and sweep floor.

Nope, Buddy did not understand sweeping perfectly good dirt off the floor.

Grandma and Annie headed back in. Buddy walked them to the house.

"You be a good boy, Buddy," Annie said, and tiny arms wrapped around his giant, oversized head.

Buddy liked hugs. They made him feel good all over.

He lay down on the back porch.

Ahhhh.

Three hours later, Buddy was returning from patrol – all was quiet, the front to the back forty. All was in order. He had stopped at Icky Springs to give a few barks to the neighbor dogs, just enough to send them into a tizzy. That little one, the shih zu, was still going strong, twenty minutes later – *yap, yap, yap, yap, yap.*

"I've never heard anything more annoying," Buddy mumbled to himself.

He came around the corner of the barn, along the grassy lane, next to the chicken coop, and who should be there, loitering – appearing to smoke a cigarette – but Kitty.

Kitty Cat.

"How ya doin', Cat?"

Buddy wasn't too crazy about being cordial to a cat, but, as Grandma said, she was part of the family, too.

"I'm doin' all right, mister," Kitty replied.

Kitty had a way of talking like an old time gangster, like she thought she was Bonnie Parker or something: girl gone bad.

Buddy wasn't much for small talk, particularly with a cat.

"So," he said, "the dogs, those maniacs from next door, they say you've been coming around too much, lately. I don't get it. Why do you gotta go over there, anyway? You got two-hundred and forty acres here."

Kitty shrugged. She held her head cocked and low, like she might be wearing a narrow-brimmed fedora and a trench coat, maybe standing under a streetlamp in a Bogart movie.

"I like ta spread myself around, bub."

"Yeah, well, they're giving me problems. That beagle –"

"Da beagle is a mo-ron," Kitty interjected. "He t'inks he's smarter 'n everyone else. He's da one runnin' da show over d'ere, ya know."

"I figured as much," Buddy replied. "But how do you know that?"

"I've heard 'em over d'ere. Hmph," Kitty snorted. "Beagle Boy don't just come right out and say it, but believe me, d'ere's only one dog in control over d'ere, and it ain't that dope, Vic."

"He is a dope, isn't he?"

"Ya got d'at right, buster."

"So," Buddy said, "you're out every night. You see everything that's going on."

"Yeah? So?"

"Well, how come you don't keep watch?"

"Keep watch? What'a'ya talkin' about, keep watch?"

19

"I'm serious. Keep watch. You know, at night?"

"What? Ya got a screw loose up d'ere?"

"Look, Done-did has been giving me grief over it. He says his hens are in a dither."

"A dither? He said dither?"

"Yeah, dither. Anyway, he's got a point. I mean –"

"Look, buster," Kitty said, looking around suspiciously, like in an old black and white movie. "I got enough on my plate with all d'ese mice … Get it? On my plate? Mice?"

"I'm not sayin' ya confront them. Just let out a bark or two."

"Bark?"

"I mean, sound the alarm, you know? Meow loud. Or something."

Kitty seemed to think about it.

Then she said, "Get out'a here."

SQUEEEEEEEEEEK!!

Buddy's ears perked. His spirits soared.

The school bus!

Buddy did just as Kitty said; he got out of there, big, brown paws propelling him down the green grassy lane, towards the County Road.

*   *   *

SQUEEEEEEEEEEK!!

Davy cringed. He wished they would fix the brakes on old Bus No. 9.

As the red signal-arm came back in and the bus ground through one gear after another, Davy kept his eyes fastened ahead. He knew the exact spot that he would see Buddy, sitting by the gate, staring in his direction, his tail wagging furiously.

And there he was.

"Good boy," Davy mumbled under his breath.

His eyes never left the big, brown dog until –

SQUEEEEEEEEEEK!!

Davy cringed.

The signal-arm went out. He walked up the aisle, punched a boy in the arm, got kicked in the butt, laughed, said goodbye to Mrs. Dietz, and got off the bus.

School was officially over for today. Oh, joy!

A boy's joy.

What could be better?

A boy's and his dog's joy, that's what.

"Woof!"

"Don't pee your pants, Buddy," Davy said as he opened and shut the gate.

20

Even at this early stage, an awful lot of Pappy had worn off on Davy.

Then came the big reunion: lots of wagging, hugging, and slobbery dog spit.

"So, how was your day today, Buddy?"

Great!

With that, boy and dog loped in joyous accord up the grassy lane, towards home. Davy was humming a tune, whatever tune happened to be in his head, but with the lyrics, "Buddy Boy, Buddy Boy, Buddy, Buddy, Buddy Boy."

"You know, Buddy?" Davy said. "Pappy's right. The Buddy Boy song can be sung to just about any tune."

That's what I hear.

*   *   *

"What are all these flies doin' in here?" Pappy queried, passing through, off for his afternoon sojourn to the hot bathtub.

"Grandma wants more flies in the kitchen," Annie replied, "so the gecko doesn't starve to death."

"Oh, yeah, the gecko." Pappy glanced at the window sill. "Well, I think there's enough flies in here now."

He looked at the plant on the window sill – Grandma's teeny, tiny, inside garden.

"Why don't you just take the pot outside and shake it out? If he's in there, he'll fall out," he suggested.

"What?!" Grandma said, incredulous. "And ruin his little house?"

"But," Pappy wondered out loud. "Didn't you say you wanted to catch him and let him go outside? Wouldn't that be ... taking him from his house?"

Pappy paused. He looked at Davy, Annie, and Grandma, and he said, "You ... don't want him to leave, do you?"

"He's so cute," Grandma replied, and she set a fresh bottlecap of water on the window sill for him.

"So," Pappy said, "what if you cracked the window and the screen, then the little fella could come and go as he pleases? You know, go out with the guys, maybe find a cute little gecko gal."

The other faces in the room appeared impressed, once again, with Pappy's wisdom, resourcefulness, and laser-like focus.

A while later, the fire was going under the bathtub, the water warm enough for entry. He took one last look around to make sure no one was looking – and they should not be, everyone being fully aware that it was Pap's hot bathtub time and to look could leave them with permanent eye or psychological brain damage.

The coast clear, he whipped off his skivvies and hopped in. Grandma said Pap could move pretty fast, for an old fella.

Ahhhhh!

A little while later, Pappy was all settled in, mumbling the Buddy Boy song and working on his new novel, based on his great-great-grandpappy's experiences on the Florida prairie.

"Hurry up!"

He was waiting for a bee to finish having a drink of his beer.

He squinted. "I see you there under the porch, Buddy! Layin' around with that armadilly."

I'm not with *the armadilly! He, or she, just* happens *to be nearby!*

Pappy settled back into the hot, flame-broiling water.

"Hm," he mumbled. "Nothin' better than a good dog snoozin' under my porch."

Chapter Three

Buddy didn't have time to be out there, having fun with Pap. No, he was hard at work, getting the sand under the porch just right, building a wall between him and the armadillo. It was almost done.

Pappy had put up a new, intricate trap system next to the porch. The last seventeen attempts had failed. One time they'd had the armadillo in the trap, but he had somehow escaped.

"Now, how in tarnation did he get out of there?" Pappy had said, scratching his head. "You can see where he tore up the ground under the trap, but … how did he get out of there? He must have opened the door … somehow."

Buddy had scratched his own head on that one. That was one tough – or smart – armadillo. Either way, it kind of made him kind of nervous.

Anyway, the wall of sand would work fine. Buddy didn't want any cooties or leprosy or whatever, seeping over from his, her, side.

Finally, he finished. An impermeable wall of sand separated him from the homely scourge. Buddy gave it the once over, nodded approvingly, then headed back out.

*   *   *

"Ya might as well come on over and hang with old Pap, Buddy!"

A lot was going on.

The mockingbirds were going at it lately, especially this time of day. Their latest fledgling couldn't get the message that it was time to strike out on his own.

"I know how you feel," Pap mumbled. "Ya boot the yaps out the one door, they come right back in the other."

He was making adjustments to his bristly "scrub-brush-poker-thing," a homemade, extendable, double-ended, combination scrub brush/coal poker, for keeping the fire under his hot bathtub at the perfect temperature.

Pappy's eyes traced to Grandma's birdfeeder. "See that, Big Boy?"

Big Boy was the oversized anole that lived near Pappy's hot bathtub, in the outgrowth of mother-in-law tongues that grew nearby.

"You know," Pappy went on, "catbirds aren't that bright. Why, they can't even figure out how to use a birdfeeder. See that? All the other birds, they're comin' and goin', chowing down – cardinals, buntings, doves, jays, sparrows – and none of them have a problem – only those catbirds." He paused. "And what's with the mockingbirds, anyway? They can't be bothered? Is the birdfeeder beneath them?"

Buddy came out from under the porch.

"Hey, Buddy!" Pappy shouted. "You finally find the time to come sit with your good, old host of hosts."

Pappy smiled as Buddy headed his way. Then he scowled as the screen door slammed and Buddy made an about face.

"Hmph," Pappy grumbled.

But it was all right. Davy was heading his direction, Buddy right behind.

Pap gave Buddy a look, and grumbled, "Hmph."

Sorry. Buddy shrugged. *It was a choice between a boy with cookies or an old man in a hot bathtub doling out drops of beer.*

"You're lucky to get that," Pappy mumbled. "Maw says no beer at all.

Hmph.

"Hmph."

*   *   *

"So, Pap," Davy said. "What's going on?" He sat down on the stool placed near, but not too near, the bathtub.

"Oh, not much. Just wonderin' why Buddy would prefer a kid with a cookie over me, his lord and most benevolent benefactor." Pappy sighed and made a face of woe. "My own disloyal, royal hound."

"He's not disloyal, Pap," Davy giggled. "Not if you're a cookie. Right, Buddy?"

Buddy gazed faithfully at the cookie.

"Here you go," Davy said. He gave him a piece.

It appeared a thought passed through Pappy's mind.

"You know," he said. "I been thinkin'."

Davy liked it when Pappy said that. There was never any telling what might come out of his mouth.

"Well, me and Buddy was talkin' the other day, and I was sayin' it might be the grandkids should start callin' him Uncle Buddy."

"Uncle Buddy? Oh, I get it. If he's like your son, he would be like my uncle, right?"

"Exactly," Pappy said.

"And Kitty should be Aunt Kitty?"

"Sounds right to me," Pappy said, pushing his straw hat back. "And Uncle Star, and Uncle Oke, too!"

Davy giggled. "Grandma's right, Pap. You're crazy."

24

Pap looked around – cunningly, plottingly – and mumbled, "That's crazy like a loon, kid. If ya know what I'm sayin'."

Davy laughed. "Oh, I know what you're saying, Pap. So," he asked, "how come you don't mind Buddy digging under the porch, but you do the armadillo?"

"Well, for one, because Buddy don't dig all the way to China so the house tumbles down the hole and we all have to learn Chinese and start eating with chopsticks. And number two, it's an armadilly! They can carry leprosy, you know."

"That's what I heard," Davy said, "somewhere."

Pappy nodded over his shoulder at the barn.

"Oke won't come out of his stall today."

"Uh-oh. Did he get his legs shaved again?"

"Yep. And I can feel for the little guy. He looks pretty ridiculous."

"He sure does," Davy concurred.

They sat like that a while and talked about school. Davy didn't mention the fight he got into that day.

"So, Grandma didn't mention anything about that fat lip of yours?"

"No. I kept my head turned."

"Michael Yaruso again?"

"Yeah."

Pappy sighed, but said nothing.

Davy was aware that Pappy was not supposed to give advice about "altercations." Anyway, Davy knew what that advice was. Everyone knew what it was, which was why Pappy was "discouraged" from giving said advice. If Pappy were to give advice, however, it would be to go in swinging from out of nowhere and make the offender, the bully in this case, "ponder real hard" before picking on someone the next time.

"I'm gonna try it," Davy declared. "You wait and see."

They locked eyes. Pappy said nothing, and Davy could see that he was on his side.

Buddy, too.

"So," Pappy said, taking a drink of beer, dolloping a drop or two for Buddy. "It looks like Mammy has bunting aplenty at her birdfeeder this year."

Davy snickered. "And squirrels aplenty, too. Cousin Charles says Grandma's gonna wear out her broom chasing them away."

Pappy shook his head. "Gotta tell ya, kid. We got all these dadblamed birds waddlin' 'round the property now. Can't hardly fly, they're so fat. And now it's the squirrels. I told her, she's gonna turn the Last Resort into a squirrel farm if she ain't careful."

"I think she's starting to notice you might be right."

Pappy shrugged. "And now, because there's so many squirrels, the hawk, he's gonna get fat, too; and there's probably gonna be more of 'em comin' around because of all the fat squirrels; and we're gonna end up with a whole farm full of overweight birds, squirrels, and hawks, all of 'em too fat to fly and waddlin' around all over tarnation!"

"Yep," Davy sighed. "I can see it now."

*   *   *

Davy and Buddy headed out front to the treehouse to play with the other kids. There wasn't much to do there for Buddy but look up and bark, so he was heading back to see what was going on with Pappy.

"Now that is a *loyal*, royal hound," Pappy commented upon his arrival.

Aw, come on, Pap. I've got things to do, people to see, places to go, just like you.

"Actually, I don't have a lot of people to see or a lot of places to go," Pap said, picking up his pencil. "Now, let's see," he mumbled, "where was I? Oh, yeah. Billy Hackensaw and Great-great-grandfather Loxley were bringing the new school teacher back from Tampa. What was her name? It's in Aunt Becky's diary. Oh, yes. Madeline. Madeline O'Dell. Now how did that story go?"

He looked off in the distance, then wrote something down. He read it over, then chuckled.

"Boy, oh, boy," Pap mumbled to himself. "This is gonna be a best seller, no doubt about that!"

Buddy rolled over and groaned. Big sigh.

"What is it, old pal?"

It's uh, it's Done-did. He's complaining about the raccoons again. He thinks we should have twenty-four hour security.

"Look, Buddy. You know Maw's not gonna let you go runnin' off at night. We've talked about this."

I know. But I told him I'd talk to you about it. And it would be nice, I gotta tell you.

"Well, that coop is just fine," Pap said. "The hens are safe in there."

I suppose, but I wanted to mention I ... had a dream.

"About the chicken coop?"

No, a doggie door. I dreamed we had a doggie door, and I came and went on my own – daylight hours only, of course – and no one ever had to hold the door for me ever again – during the day.

Buddy eyed Pappy. He could read him pretty well by now.

"Hm," Pappy said. "A doggie door would be nice. Why, sometimes I think the only reason I have hands is to open and close that door for you."

Buddy shrugged.

"I gotta tell ya," Pappy mumbled. "That might be a good idea. And I know just the place to put it, too, over there on that side door, goes into the mudroom."

Sounds good to me, Pap.

"Yeah. I'll bring it up to Maw. Speaking of which," Pappy said, "what is it she's doing in there? Can you see? She's ... what is that she's doing?"

Hm. Buddy studied the situation. *It looks like she's doing something by the kitchen window.*

"Well, I can see that. What's that she's doin', though?"

*   *   *

Grandma was on a mission.

"What are you doing, Mother?"

"Yeah. What are you doing, Grandma?"

"Yeah, Grandma. What are you doing?"

Grandma didn't reply. She was busy taking the screen out of the window.

Uncle Kenny walked in the kitchen. "What's she doin'?"

Everyone shrugged.

She got the screen loose and let it drop onto the porch deck. Everyone gathered around.

Cousin Vicki Lynn walked in. "What's going –"

"Shhhh!"

Cousin Vicki Lynn joined the others, watching. A squirrel hopped onto the porch rail, then leaped out, up, and onto the birdfeeder.

The suspense was deafening.

You could hear a rolling-pin drop as Grandma loaded her pistol – with water – then got into firing position. The twins walked in.

"What's –"

"Shhhh."

Grandma took aim. Careful aim. And ... FIRE!!

Everyone held their breath as she loosed round after round ... ... and the squirrel ignored her.

Alas. Grandma just didn't have the range. Grandma's stream was weak.

The gathered let out a piteous sigh. They went to her to comfort her, but Grandma turned, and with a stalwart, pioneer-type, I-can-overcome look in her eye.

She mumbled, "Darn it."

27

All could clearly see that it was not over, though. She still had "gumption in her gut," as Pappy would say. In a moment of reckless rage, she spun on her heel, jumped up and down, waved her arms, and shouted, "GET OUT OF HERE! GET! YEEAAAHHHHHH!!"

But the squirrel, that wicked but oh-so-cute rodent, only stared right through her, as if she weren't there at all.

She turned again, and all could see: It was over. Grandma was beaten. She stared despondently at her plastic squirt gun, a look of defeat and helplessness in her eyes.

But then, as if a blessing from above, little Annie said, "You know what you need, Grandma? You need a Supersoaker."

All grew quiet as Grandma tilted her head. She lifted a curious eyebrow.

"Supersoaker?" she said. "What's a ... Supersoaker?"

*   *   *

"What is that woman of mine doin' in there?"

I can't say for sure, Pap, but I think she's shooting a squirt gun out the window at the squirrels.

"Huh. Imagine that."

Yeah. Imagine that.

Chapter Four

Dusk was a busy part of the day for Marv. Mabel would expect plenty of high-flying, heartfelt singing, bidding all a good, long goodnight. Mabel had been impressed with her new additions of broom straw. It looked like she was in a fine mood for a nice, quiet – possibly romantic – evening at home.

Ah, the home life.

Marv was up on his telephone pole, closing the day out, keeping everyone on the farm entertained with his expansive repertoire and eloquent delivery. The man, Pappy, got out of the hot bathtub and headed in, which was the signal that the day was almost over. It was almost time to settle in for the night.

Ah, the home life.

Then all came to ruin. There he was. He was back. Junior.

He flew over and perched on the telephone line.

"Hey, Pop. How ya doin'?"

Big sigh. "I'm fine."

"So, how's Mom?"

"She's fine, too. Just been getting the nest back in order … a nest made for two, I might add," Marv noted, hoping Junior got the idea.

"Oh," he said, "maybe I'll stop in and see how she's doin."

"Look … son," Marv said. "You moved out a week ago. Remember? It's the way of the world. You have to go off and make your own life now, son. We would be irresponsible as parents if we let you mooch … uh, I mean, if we didn't encourage you to make a life of your own."

"Aw, come on, Pop. Why can't I live here? I love it here. Why can't we be like the scrub jays? They never have to leave home. Barry says it's just one big happy family over there."

"Hmph," Marv grumbled. "I don't think it's as lovey-dovey over there as they make you think. Have you heard some of those knockdown, drag-outs? Late at night?"

Junior frowned. "Come on, Pop. It's just for tonight. I … I haven't really gotten around to building a nest yet. Betty and Veronica are keeping me pretty busy these days, you know."

"But, son," Marv sighed. "How do you plan to find a nice girl without a decent nest? It takes work, son. You've seen me at it. Why, just today I brought your mother some first rate broom straw. It's completely changed the dining room. It really opens it up."

"Oh!" Junior said. "Can I see it?!"

Marv scowled.

"I mean," Junior went on, "it would really give you a chance to show me some of your workbirdship."

Marv noticed Mabel looking out the window.

"You'll have to excuse me, son, but I have a job to do."

With that, Marv paused from his churrish conversation with Junior and belted out a smooth rendition of "Yellow Submarine."

It was hard, though, watching Junior flit off to "visit" with his ma.

Marv grumbled under his breath, "He just better not leave the toilet seat up or his dirty socks in the middle of the floor."

*   *   *

The big, old, oak tree in the front yard was a busy place. It was home to many, from frogs and lizards to birds and, yes, squirrels. The Darwin family.

They had been living here a long time; since the old days even.

There had been times over the years that squirrels from the forest had tried to move in, and in an unneighborly fashion. The Darwins had held out, however, keeping the invaders at bay, thus ensuring that their descendants would forever flourish in this grand, old, oak tree on the front lawn of the house on the grassy lane.

The family patriarch was Chuck. Chuck Darwin.

He didn't leave the tree much anymore, but he had tales to tell.

Problem was, young folks weren't listening these days: "Not like we used to when we were kids!" No, they had more important things to do than sit around listening to old folks spouting ancient history.

Chuck observed from his comfortable perch high in the branches. It happened every now and then, there would be a long dry spell. The birdfeeder would sit empty, bereft of munchy delights. Then, one day, it would all of a sudden be overflowing with seeds, grain, and nuts.

Then, and only then, would a new generation take to the field of battle.

Chuck observed the activity on the ground, between the tree and the porch. They had not seen any sign of the woman, Grandma, lately, not since the last time she stormed out onto the porch with the broom.

It never got old, watching the young folks taunt the woman with the broom.

"Oh, look!" Daphne shouted, pointing at the kitchen window.

"What is that she's doing?" Miguel wondered out loud.

They all watched with interest as the screen popped out of the window and fell to the porch decking.

"Yo, dude. Like, what's she doin' in there?" Halsey asked no one in particular.

"Who is that down there, at the feeder?" Chuck asked, taking his glasses off to clean them.

"It's Artie," Micco replied. "And," he suddenly cried, "Grandma's got a gun!"

"Oh, my gosh! A gun!" someone else shouted.

"Artie! Get out of there!" everyone chattered. "Get out of there!"

But it was too late. Artie, the community's best acrobat and birdfeeder knocker-overer, was fully involved in getting a stuck peanut from jamming the feeder tray.

"ARTIE!" Everyone cried.

But it was too late. He heard them and looked up just in time to see Grandma in the kitchen window, the gun pointed right at him!

Some of the onlookers closed their eyes as Artie froze, like a deer caught with its pants down. It burned from Grandma's eyes, the rage, the ill intent; and she did not hesitate. She fired.

Squirt!

She fired again. *Squirt!*

And again. *Squirt!*

And now everyone knew: Grandma had a weak stream.

There arose a patter of amusement at first, then laughter, then full-blown hilarity as she continued to fire. Artie put his tail in the air and wiggled his butt. He stuck his thumbs in his ears and waggled his fingers.

Even old Chuck, from up on his comfy perch, laughed.

"Oh!" he declared to all. "This will be a story for the ages!"

Yes, everyone in the tree, not just the Darwin family but all the other residents, and their guests, enjoyed the moment.

Artie, meanwhile, got the birdfeeder swinging in a good, wide arc, causing lots of seed and grain to fall to the ground below. A minute later, the ground swarmed with squirrels and birds, even those from the trees out in the pasture and the orange grove across the grassy lane.

It seemed a time for fun and celebration. Then, all of a sudden, the Dutch door slammed open and around the corner charged Grandma, broom in hand, and looking like she meant business, too. Squirrels and birds both scattered in all directions.

Here she came, like Henry V himself, her battle axe held high over her head. Over the rail she leaped. Into the yard she charged, clearing the field of combatants, all of them scattering to the four winds or up the tree, from where they gathered to observe as she ran around below and hurled insults and threats.

Finally, she tired of the battle and retreated to her castle walls.

A few minutes later, a lone squirrel ventured down the tree and across the yard. He stopped to munch on a nice, juicy peanut, waved triumphantly to the others, then dashed over to the croton bush, hopped up onto the porch rail, wiggled his butt at the kitchen window, and made an impressive leap out, up, and over to the birdfeeder.

From the tree erupted a rousing round of applause for Artie Darwin.

He took a bow, and all knew it was safe to venture forth onto the field of victory, thus reaping and enjoying their rightful spoils of war.

*   *   *

"That woman of mine, she's pretty fast, huh?" Pappy noted from his watery throne.

I'd say. Buddy concurred.

"And that broom. Kind'a scary, if ya ask me?"

I hope I never get on her bad side.

"Me neither."

Chapter Five

Elwood O. Possum yawned grandly, exposing a mouthful of sharp, white teeth. He rolled over and smacked his thin lips.

He looked out the end of his hollowed, cabbage palm log – a really nice location along the edge of the orange grove, just down and across the grassy lane from the big house. It looked like the sun was going down.

Time to get up and go to work.

He crawled out of his house and took time for a good, long stretch and yawn.

Elwood thought he'd take his regular route, down to the lake to start things off, maybe scoop up a lazy fish or crawdad. There was always some sort of tasty bug or whatnot down there. Then he'd work his way up to the barn and see if Bundy Mac, the rat snake, might have left him a mouse to munch on. If not, there were always slugs and palmetto bugs around.

Elwood adored palmetto bugs, the way they crunched and all the legs squiggled when he bit into them.

The eventual destination, of course, was the two sets of garbage cans, one at the barn, the other up at the house. That was the one most likely *not* to be closed properly. Sometimes, there wouldn't be a lid on it at all, if one of the kids took the garbage out last. Elwood thanked his lucky stars for forgetful, irresponsible kids. Last night had been Greek night ... HEY!

He didn't want to dillydally. The racoons would be along later.

Elwood thought raccoons on the dim side. They did not understand the importance of stealth and quiet when foraging for sustenance. They came in like gangbusters, tossing things around and making a big racket. That kind of behavior shed a bad light on those more peaceable of mind, and practical, like Elwood, those who just wanted to do their job, and then go home. No, the racoons had to put on a big show, every night, marching around and being rude and unruly.

But that was a good thing about raccoons, Elwood supposed. He could always hear them coming. He never wanted to be around when they got there either, especially whenever the man, Pappy, stuck his shotgun out the window and opened fire.

Talk about a racket.

No, for Elwood, it was all about the job. He thought he could maybe save a little cash so he could move up to a nicer place, maybe meet a nice girl, settle down, and live the American dream.

He was doing pretty good tonight. The crawdads were delicious. He was just coming around the corner of the barn, next to the chicken coop, when he froze. The cat! Not a muscle moved. Cats could be trouble. Hardly a breath escaped his lips. She was intent on a rat skulking along the back wall of the barn.

Elwood was a master of "Freeze!" While in that frozen position, waiting for Kitty to catch the rat or move on or whatever, he kept himself busy by doing anagrams and palindromes in his head.

A while later, the coast was clear. Elwood continued on. He was coming around the other corner of the barn, heading along the fence-line towards the house, when who should walk around the end of the fence but the dog.

Their eyes locked, and Elwood instantly keeled over onto his side, teeth bared, eyes wide open and glassy – the universal pose of dead possum.

He watched as the big dog, Buddy, walked over and sniffed.

Oh, sheesh. Inner sigh. *Here we go again.*

It was tough for Elwood, keeping up the dead act as the dog picked him up in his powerful jaws and carried him off. Elwood was a professional, though, and hung limp as dog drool ran into his eyes and dripped off the pointy point of his nose.

Elwood was grateful that Buddy obviously had some retriever in him. Quite gentle, actually.

"Doesn't this ever get old?" he mumbled to himself as Buddy carried him up the five steps to the porch where the two men, Pappy and Uncle Amos, were drinking beer and telling the same old stories over and over.

P-lop!

He lay there on the deck. Dead possum. And –

Oh, sheesh. Here we go again.

"Well, look at that, Amos. Ya reckon that's the same possum Buddy brought us the other night?"

"Could be."

"Ya think he's alive?"

"Could be."

Elwood waited.

All right, all right. Let's go. Open the door; let the dog inside. You do it every time.

A second later, Pappy opened the door, and Buddy went in.

Finally. Sheesh!

With that, Elwood could finally blink.

Ah, that feels good.

34

He got up, and, as usual, Pappy tried to scare him back to "death" by jumping up and down like some bald-headed, long-bearded kook.

Elwood was not afraid of Pappy, though. He just ambled off, down the five steps and into the twilight night.

*   *   *

Buddy liked evening time, after dinner.

While the women cleaned up, Buddy and Pappy were in charge of the living room. They were watching TV with the kids.

"Are the kids allowed to watch decapitations?!" Pappy shouted.

"NO!!" from the kitchen and upstairs and down the hallway.

"All right, all right," he mumbled, flipping the station. "No need ta get all testy. Just askin'. Sorry, kids," he said. "No more decapitations. I did my best."

A minute later, little Paul asked, "Who does Buddy like best, Pappy? You or Grandma?"

"Oh, that would be me," Pappy declared, brimming with confidence. "Hands down," he said. "Right, Buddy? ... Buddy?"

Buddy had to tread lightly here. He hemmed, and he hawed. He didn't really answer.

"So," Davy queried, as if not convinced, "Buddy would come to you instead of Grandma? In a calling contest?"

Pappy made a sour face. He scratched his beard.

"A calling contest, huh?" He squirmed in his big, comfy chair. "Why," he stammered, "of course he would. Right? Buddy? ... Uh ... Buddy?"

Buddy wasn't really paying attention. He stared into the kitchen. He couldn't be sure, but it sounded like something just had landed in his bowl.

*   *   *

It was almost bedtime for the kids. Pappy was reading to them from his novel, called *The Cow Hunters*, based on their ancestors.

"Billy, Bo, and Mudge were exploring," Pappy read. "It was their favorite pastime, heading out into the unknown for days at a time, living off the land. As the boys had grown older, they traveled progressively farther from home, all the way to the big river to the west. The Kissimmee it was called. –"

A hand shot up. Little Paul. "That's the river we live on!"

"That's right," Pappy said. He continued. "They were following the river northward, in the direction of its origin – wherever that was. Mudge, meanwhile, was having his way with the cows –"

35

Another hand shot up. Little Jack.

"Mudge was the greatest cow dog to ever run the Florida range!"

"That is correct," Pappy said. He continued. "In their journeys, as the boys and their dog hiked through new country, Mudge would round up cows and herd them. By the time they neared home they'd have a dozen or more – too many to keep – so they would sometimes pick one out to take with them, and the rest they'd have Mudge disperse. This was Mudge's favorite part – the dispersing of the cows, which could take a while with the cows regrouping as fast as Mudge could scatter them. He would be off dispersing one group, then look to see another group reforming, and he would be off to disperse them.

"Finally, Billy would yell, 'Come on, Mudge!' and Mudge would run over and sit down in front of the boys with a perplexed, but hopeful, expression. The two boys could not help but laugh –"

A hand shot up. Annie.

"Mudge hopes they have a treat for him, doesn't he? Just like Buddy, huh?!"

Annie hugged Buddy.

A treat?! Buddy exclaimed. *Great! Where is it?! Gimme! Gimmie! Gimmie!*

No treat. But hugs were good, too.

Buddy rolled over for the full-belly extravaganza.

Ahhhhh!

He liked the stories of Mudge, from the old days, and the other Buddy, too. Buddy was descended from both of them, Mudge and Buddy. The one he was named for was the first Buddy to be the farm dog here. Buddy often wondered about that Buddy, what it was like to live here then, over a hundred years ago.

Buddy stretched out and enjoyed his full-belly extravaganza, and the long ago tales of Mudge; and he wondered if that had indeed been the sound of someone tossing a morsel into his bowl.

*   *   *

Everyone was off to bed. Some would resist those unassailable coils of sleep; others would revel in them. As one after another succumbed, the big old farm house itself seemed to drift and lumber into its own deep, restful, slumber.

TV time. Time for the old folks to sit back and take in the day.

Little Jack came down the stairs, rubbing his eyes.

"Where's Grandma?"

Pappy shrugged. "I think she's out in the laundry room, drinkin' beer."

"Oh, I am not!" Grandma said from the kitchen. "Don't tell him that, Pap." She stepped through the door. "What is it, sweetheart?"

"I don't feel good."

Pappy looked at Buddy. "I need ta get me some pajamas like that, with those little feet in 'em."

I could use some of those, too, Buddy mused. *They look comfy.*

"Cozy," Pappy suggested.

Oh. Cozy as heck.

Buddy listened intently for the sound of something landing in his bowl. Finally, he could stand it no longer, not with the possibility that Jack's illness might be remedied by cookies or ice cream or something like that – so he got up.

"Where ya goin'?" Pap said.

I'll be back.

A minute later, Pap followed Buddy into the kitchen. He had been right. Jack was getting ice cream for a sore throat.

Buddy was drooling.

"Oh, Buddy," Grandma sighed. She handed him a doggie treat so he'd have to lick his lips.

Works every time.

Pappy grumbled, "I might as well get my own snackeroo whilst I'm waitin' on you all."

A minute later, Jack was off to bed again. Buddy was concentrating on Pap. No one was messier in the kitchen than Pap. Buddy was sticking to him like "brown on Buddy," as Pap sometimes said.

Grandma claimed that without PBJs, Pap would have dried up and blown away a long time ago.

Buddy found the best place to stand when Pap was making his sandwich was between him and the counter. That way he didn't miss anything, unless Pap dropped jelly right on his head, which had happened before. It was worth the risk, though.

Waiting for the toast.

Grandma came back from putting Jack to bed.

Waiting for the toast.

They started talking about their day, which was fine with Buddy, except they were completely ignoring him.

Hey, what am I? Chopped liver?

Buddy hated it when they did that – talked to each other as if he weren't even in on the conversation.

"Woof!"

"And enter Sir Barks a Lot," Grandma mumbled.

Pappy gave him the look. "Hush, Buddy. We're tryin' ta talk."

And there they went again, as if his opinion did not matter.

"Woof!"

"Hush!"

Darn it.

If that wasn't bad enough, they started talking about the family, and the kids, and how blessed they were. Buddy could see it coming.

Oh, sheesh. Here we go again.

Yep, there they went. Grandma and Pappy were hugging, right there, in the middle of the kitchen, as if no one else was there.

"Woof!"

"Hush!"

"Woof, woof! Woof!"

"Hush, Buddy! Bad dog! We're tryin' to talk here!"

No, you're not. You're just standing there, hugging.

"Woof!"

As Pappy would say, desperate times call for desperate measures. So Buddy tried one more, really big, "WOOF!!"

"Hush!! Bad dog!!"

Fine, Buddy grumbled. He took matters into his own paws and barged right between them, forcing them apart with his expansive, oversized, wide-load head.

That usually got them, as it did this time.

They giggled, then kissed, and said, "All right, Buddy. You win." They patted him on the head and wondered how such a "big lug" could be "so cute."

Back to the business at hand: a PBJ and – hopefully – hurried, sloppy preparations. Jelly could fly when Pap got going – especially when he was in a rush.

Hurry up, Pap. The show's already started.

"It's your fault he's a bad dog, Pap," Grandma was saying. "You're a bad influence."

"Well," Pappy shrugged, in his way, "you knew that was a possibility when you married the bad boy."

"Bad boy," Grandma huffed. "That from the man who shares his beer with lizards and bees."

"Lizards and bees need beer, too," Pappy said. "Anyway, that's all for show. Inside I'm tortured and consumed with boundless angst and rage."

Grandma rolled her eyes.

She looked to Buddy. "Not a word from you, young man."

Buddy shut his mouth.

How did she know I was about to woof? My gosh, Pap's right. She reads minds.

"So," she asked, "I suppose you want a treat, too, Buddy?"

Oh, my gosh! She is! She's a mind reader!

Buddy was suddenly distracted by the toaster popping. There he was, in position, between Pap and the counter, looking up, ready for manna to tumble his way. One time, Pap dropped a whole stick of butter on the floor and never noticed it until Grandma said, "What happened to that brand new stick of butter?"

It had been way too late by then.

A few minutes later, all were back in the living room. Buddy was sitting loyally next to Pap, who was munching on his PBJ. Buddy always got the last corner-bite crust.

Except he realized he had to go. Real bad. All of a sudden-like. It must have been something he ate, probably whatever that was in that old lunch bag he found out by the County Road.

Hurry up, Pap! Eat your sandwich!

Finally, Pap finished. Buddy got his corner crust.

Thank goodness.

Then, *I gotta go.*

Pap gave him the look.

Sorry, Pap. I gotta go.

"Really, Buddy? Can't you wait?"

Buddy stressed that waiting was not the best option.

"Ohhh, I get it," Pappy said with a wink; and he got up to let him out, saying loudly, "I'm gettin' pert near tired 'a jumpin' up every minute for that dog! He wants in! He wants out! In, out! In, out!"

As the door opened, but before it closed, Buddy heard Pap saying, loudly, "You know what we need around here, Maw?! We need a doggy door!"

Nice goin', Pap! Buddy mumbled to himself as he hurried down the steps and out into the yard in search of the perfect place to go – someplace real close by.

Hurry up, Buddy. Hurry up. Hurry up! Hurry up!!

Chapter Six

It was late. Prowling hours.

Of anyone, everyone, at the farmhouse on the grassy lane, Kitty was the most independent. Indeed, she was the most unhampered, the most liberated of all. That would include, even, yes, Pappy.

Ha. Try bein' a cat, Mr. Liberty for All. Cats rule!

Especially Kitty. No one came and went around as freely as Kitty did.

She was still in a lather over Buddy, suggesting she be some kind of watchcat.

A watchcat? That's preposterous. There's a reason that's not a word.

Then the big-headed lug had the gall, the nerve, to suggest she should limit herself to their two hundred forty acres.

Cats need room ta roam! And two hundred forty acres is nothin', buster!

Fences are nothing for cats.

Like most felines, Kitty liked to live on the edge. The edge around here meant The Grunge, the neighbor's land, home to the notorious Sinister Six – formerly home to the nearly as notorious Fiendish Five.

It was pretty dark tonight, but not too dark. There was just enough light to see, but not be seen. Kitty was pushing the limits, having already left the cover of the woods. The Grunge wasn't anything like The Last Resort. It was, in fact, the opposite in every quantifiable way.

For starters, the house and grounds were run down and ratty – as in rats, everywhere.

Seriously, what is with da stinkin' cats over here? Some 'a d'ese t'ings are bigger d'an me!

That was another danger over here; not the dogs, but the cats. There were three of them: Greco, Guido, and Maude. They were all three lowdown, measly, and obviously lazy.

Three cats? And all these rats?

Shiftless.

Kitty moved stealthily. She prided herself on her stealth. One step at a time. Stop. Listen. Observe.

Kitty could see them in there, in their lair, under the dilapidated porch with the washing machine and junk piled everywhere. She was just outside the latticework, in the shadows, near the rusty, old, leaky, water pump. Every now and then she could hear voices from inside – Old Man Perkins yelling at Old Lady Perkins – and occasional stomping around.

"Bloody well roight," Cornwall, the overweight English hound, was saying. "Oi saw that cat over 'ere just last noight, Oi did."

"I saw her first," Ali, the fit and trim boxer, chimed in.

"Bloimey!" Cornwall responded. "Oi saw 'er first, Oi did. Remember? Oi said, 'There's that bloody cat!'"

"No. I said, 'There's that stupid cat!'"

"No, you didn't."

"Yes, I did."

"No, you –"

"*DEN MUND HALTEN*!" Vic screamed. "Bozh of you! Stifle! Ve do not care who it vas who saw zhe idiot cat first!"

Idiot cat? I take offense.

"Ay-yi-yi," Ernesto, the three-legged chihuahua, growled. "I hate that cat."

"Me, too! Me, too! Me, too! Me, too! Me, too! Me –"

"SHUT UP!" everyone screamed at Viper, the shih tzu.

Viper pouted and folded her arms.

From the other side of the latticework: *My gosh, that thing is annoying.*

A toilet flushed in the house, and the clattery old pump came on. Kitty edged closer so she could hear.

"Anyway," Lionel, the beagle, continued. "We gotta send a real message. Just running up to the fence and barking our heads off isn't gonna do it any longer. We've done all we can with that hole in the fence. It's not getting any bigger, and Ernesto and Viper having access is just not enough."

Ernesto and Viper looked at each other.

"What are you sayeeng?" Ernesto grumbled. "Are you sayeeng that we are useless? That we cannot do anytheeg?"

"Yeah!" Viper agreed. "Are you saying we can't do anything?! Can't do anything?! Can't do anything?! Can't do anything?! Can't do any –"

"SHUT UP!" everyone screamed, while from the other side of the latticework: *My gosh, that thing is annoying!*

"Proceed, *Herr* Lionel," Vic said.

"Right." Lionel glared at Ernesto and Viper. "The fact is, whether you two like it or not, you're both small. There may come a point when that is exactly what we need, someone small, but I do *not* think you two can kidnap that kid and get him back over here through that little hole. Do you?"

The two little guys frowned. They looked at each other's tiny bodies and shook their heads.

"You sure this 'ere's a good oidea," Cornwall asked. "Kidnappin' the kid and 'oldin' 'im for ransom?"

"Not for ransom," Lionel said, "but to teach those high and mighty Last Resorters a lesson."

"And what ees that lesson?" Ernesto asked.

"Why," Lionel replied, "that they better figure out a way to keep that lousy cat of theirs on their side of the fence, that's what. We gotta show them that they can't push us around any longer." Lionel glanced at Vic, "Uh, right? … Vic?"

"*Ya'vol*," Vic, who was chewing on a hangnail, said. "Ve can all agree zhat ve must do somezhing. I mean, who does zhat cat zhink she is anyvay?"

"Yeah," Ali agreed, "who does that cat think she is anyvay? I mean anyway?"

Kitty could not believe what she was hearing.

Kidnapping?! How can this be?!

"Oi got a oidea," Cornwall offered. "Oi saw a episode of Law and Order, Oi did, and they 'ad a bleedin' 'ostage swap. They did."

"Hostage swap?" Ali asked.

"That's right!" Lionel said. "I saw that episode, too! Good idea, Cornster. We exchange the kid for the cat. They'd much rather have the kid than that dolt-faced cat."

Dolt-faced? Kitty was incensed.

"*Ya'vol*," Vic gushed, rubbing his nimble, thoroughly Teutonic paws together, "I like zhat. Zhe kid for zhe cat."

"And," Lionel added, "we can stick it to those stinkin' Last Resorters. So," he went on. "We need to figure out a way to lure, yes, lure that kid over here. Once we have him, there's no way he's getting away."

Lionel laughed diabolically. It sent a shiver down Kitty's spine.

The pump came on again. Kitty scowled. She inched closer. They were speaking in low tones, making plans, details.

It can happen to the best of stealthers. Maybe Kitty was being careless. Who wouldn't be, having just learned such distressing news? Kitty liked Davy. He always gave her bites of his roast beef sandwich. She did not want him kidnapped.

She moved closer, and she made that fated misstep, on a dry, brittle twig.

Snap!

She froze.

"What was that?!" Ali cried as twelve ears grew pointed, and six faces looked in her direction. Black noses sniffed the air. Then –

"GET HER!!" and a chorus of raging barks, howls, whines, arfs, and ruffs assaulted the air.

Kitty ran for it. Oh, she ran like she never ran before. She could hear them back there, Lionel and Cornwall baying madly, the others barking ferociously, and the sounds of twenty-three paws tearing at the ground behind her.

Not once did she look back. She could sense the big ones, someone, crashing through the forest, ever closer as she dashed under logs and over branches. They were right behind her. She couldn't believe how fast they were! She considered dashing up a tree, but then she'd be stuck over here.

Anyway, there was the fence-line! Right ahead!

She thought she could make it, but then, right in front of her appeared a huge, snarling Vic. He had taken a shortcut!

The others were coming up behind. She was trapped. Trapped!

"Pssst! Over here."

"Huh?" Kitty looked, and there was a small, pointy nose and beady eyes peering up from a hole in the ground.

"This way. Hurry."

There was no time to think or consider the possibilities of cooties or leprosy. Kitty dashed down the hole.

Gasping for air, she turned to see the armadillo blocking the entrance. She could see past him, to the Sinister Six glaring down into the hole at her, murder in their eyes – but something else as well.

Hesitancy.

"You want the cat," the armadillo said, "you gotta get past me first."

The big dogs looked at the little ones, and Lionel said, "Here's your chance, little guys. Go get 'er!"

But the two little guys just stared.

Finally, Ernesto said, "But … eet ees a armadillo. Eet has leprosy. And cooties, too."

"Yeah!" Viper agreed. "Cooties! Cooties! Cooties! Cooties! Coot –"

"Shut up!" everyone, including the armadillo, screamed at Viper.

"Oh!" Viper folded her arms. "I am *not* goin' in there."

Kitty, of course, was horrified at the thought of cooties or leprosy. It felt suddenly stuffy and close – and icky – in the hole.

Luckily, the armadillo said, "Go on. I'll hold them off for you."

Kitty didn't have to be told twice. She bolted the other direction, down the long tunnel until, finally, she could see moonlight ahead. She scurried out, into fresh air.

Hoo! D'at is one long, creepy ride.

She looked around. She was hidden in a clump of saw palmetto, way away from the fence; but she could see them over there still, staring down into the armadillo hole, the two little guys, paws on hips, still refusing to chase after her.

Kitty felt grateful, of course; but she also felt dirty. She needed a bath.

A moment later, the armadillo popped his hideous, goofy-looking head out of the hole.

"Hi," he said. "I'm Harlan." He extended his hand for a friendly shake.

Kitty stared at it, the dirty nails, the possibility of cooties or leprosy, and mumbled, "Uh, yeah ... nice ta meet ya, mister. Uh ... I gotta go."

And off she dashed, heading back to the house for a good, long bath.

She had a lot to think about.

Buddy would want to know of the threats to Davy. Yet Kitty did not want him, or anyone else, to think she, Kitty, could in any way be characterized as anything related or similar to a ... watchcat.

A watchcat? Really?

It could be enough to ruin a reputation.

Chapter Seven

Pappy and Buddy were staring down the hole under the porch.

"Is he in there?"

I don't know.

"What do you mean you don't know? You live down there with him, or her, don't you?"

No, I don't. Number one, I do not live *down there! Number two, we are separated by an impenetrable wall of sand. And number three, I do* not *go over there, and he, or she, does* not *come over to my side – I hope.*

"I think he, or she, is long gone," Pappy said. "There's no way he, or she, could have gotten past this latest barricade we constructed, you think? I mean, he does not look like much of a leaper – even if he is an outstanding leper." He paused. "Get it? Leaper? Leper?"

I do. Good one, Pap. Anyway, I think he, or she, must have vamoosed before we set the trap last night.

With that, Man and Dog high-fived, did a jubilant jig, and celebrated their victory with beer – just a dollop or two for Buddy, of course.

"So, I talked ta Maw about the doggy door, and she says as long as you're in at night, and you don't come traipsin' through the kitchen all day long, we can get ya one."

Really?!

"That's right, little buddy. Ya see there? Now, who's watchin' out for ya, huh?"

You are, Pap. Nice goin'. You're the best!

"Aw shucks," Pappy said. "It's nothin'."

The afternoon was spent going to town and getting the doggie door, then installing it in the mudroom door. Once complete, the rest of the afternoon was spent with the kids calling Buddy in and out of his new door, and the kids themselves going in and out of the new door.

Pappy was proud. Buddy, too.

Grandma raised an eyebrow, and said, "This has trouble written all over it."

Pap, Buddy, and all the kids could only stare back, all uniformly wondering: What can possibly go wrong?

*   *   *

"Pappy says us kids should call Buddy 'Uncle Buddy' from now on, or else we're being disrespectful to our elder."

The women and girls, aunts and cousins, were gathered in the kitchen, preparing to prepare dinner. That is, they were sitting around the table, yakking it up.

Aunt Charlotte rolled her eyes.

"Number one, young lady, Buddy is a dog. He is *not* your uncle. Number two, Buddy is actually younger than you. Either way, it is completely ridiculous for you to call him 'Uncle Buddy.'"

Annie was ready, however, and quickly replied, "Not in dog years. Pappy says Buddy is old enough in dog years that he can drink beer now. He's been around; he's experienced life that us kids have not; and he has earned our respect by protecting our house from vandals and burglars night and day for all these years."

The aunts and cousins laughed. Aunt Charlotte set her hand on her hip.

"Whatever," she said, waving her hand. She glanced at Grandma, who wiped her grin from her face.

Annie sat in her chair, next to the window, nibbling on an after school cookie. Her legs swung in a rhythmic motion as she observed the proceedings. Annie had learned that if she was quiet and inconspicuous, people forgot she was there, and they would utter things they might otherwise not.

Cousin Mary Ann was wiping down the kitchen sink when she looked out the window, and exclaimed, "What in the world is Pappy doing out there?!"

Annie spun around in her seat.

"It looks like he's got a bee or a wasp stuck in his beard again."

Instantly, women and girls crowded around the window. They laughed and howled with delight until –

"Oh, my gosh! He's getting out!"

Women and girls screamed in horror and ran away.

*　　　*　　　*

Buddy was relaxing in his nice, cool, damp-sand hole under the porch.

Ahhhhh.

He could see Pap out there through the latticework; he had just gotten back into the hot bathtub after doing battle with a bee. Or wasp.

Ahhhhh. Cool and damp.

It had been great, the doggie door. Buddy and the kids must have gone through it a thousand times today, until Aunt Charlotte declared, "No more!" and she had flipped the lock on it so they could not use it anymore. A little while later, Grandma had come and flipped it back and told Buddy to be a good boy.

Buddy had learned his lesson. From now on, he would use it sparingly, like Pap had said. Still, all Buddy could think about was trying it out again. He liked the way it flapped behind him. Pap had said it was like having a new car. At first you just want to use it a lot, even if that means just going out and sitting in it in the driveway. A novelty, he called it.

Novelties get old.

Buddy was off in doggie dream land. In his dream he was going in and out of the house whenever he wanted, in and out, in and out, in and out.

Scratch, scratch, scratch.

Some alien abstraction had invaded his dream. What was that scratching noise, like someone digging nearby? Slowly, he opened his eyes. As he did, he realized some one was staring back at him, from only inches away. Tiny, beady eyes stared, a tiny, pointy nose sniffed.

Am I dreaming? Is this a nightmare?

Eyes opened wider, and horror flooded Buddy's senses, for staring him right in the face was the armadillo.

The ... armadilly?!

Yes. He, or she, had burrowed right through Buddy's impervious wall of sand and was sniffing at him, only inches away.

Cooties! Leprosy!! Oh, the shame!!!

"Hi! I'm Harlan!"

AHHHHHHHHHH!!! Without so much as a goodbye, or an *adios*, or even a *sayonara*, Buddy was in full skedaddle, up and out from under the porch and at Pappy's side in an instant, at the hot bathtub. He panted heavily.

"What's wrong, Buddy?" Pappy asked.

It's, Buddy stammered. *It's ... it's the armadilly! He's ... she's ... whatever it is, it's ... it's still in there! And he, or she, it ... it broke through the impervious wall of sand!*

Pappy frowned. "You sure it was him ... or her?"

Buddy was incredulous.

Are you kidding me?! he cried. *Yes. Yes! It was ... it was ... ... devastating!!*

Luckily for Buddy, Pappy was there to comfort him. He rested his hand on Buddy's giant head, and said, "How's about a dollop, old pal?"

I, Buddy stammered, *I ... I suppose. And maybe ... cough ... one or two of those hot and spicey pork rinds over there, if you don't mind.*

That evening

It was raining out. It was not a hard rain; hard enough to get wet, though.

Pap and Uncle Amos were on the front porch, telling the same old stories, drinking Schlitz.

"Hard to get these things these days."

"Uncle Mo ordered 'em special."

"Catch that armadilly yet?"

"No. I think the problem is he's too smart for me and Buddy."

"And how about you know who? Trouble with the squirrels still?"

"Yep. Mm-hm. Woman wants a Supersoaker."

"Supersoaker, huh?"

"Mm-hm. She's on a mission."

"Well then, I suppose I should be there for that, when it happens."

"Mm-hm. I'll have Davy let ya know."

"So, Davy got in a fight again, huh? Saw him out by the barn earlier."

"Yep. Mm-hm."

"That fat kid again?"

"Michael Yaruso. Davy says he's gonna try the 'windmill in a hurricane' method next time."

"Always worked for you."

"Yep. Mm-hm. Little guys' specialty."

"Well, lookee there," Uncle Amos said, nodding.

They watched as the big, brown dog trod up the porch steps.

"You reckon that's the same possum he brought home last time?"

"Don't know. Looks like it."

"It sure do, don't it?"

"Yep. Mm-hm."

*   *   *

Pappy opened the door. Buddy went inside.

Elwood blinked.

Ahhhhh. That feels good.

He got up to leave. Pappy leaped to his feet and tried to scare him back to death, as usual.

Elwood ignored Pappy, though, as usual. He didn't really like the rain, so he went over to the corner of the porch and lay down to wait for it to stop. He listened to the two men discuss whether they should try to scare him to death again.

Soon, he drifted off to sleep.

When he awoke, he was alone. It was raining harder.

He sighed and lay back down. Then, out of the corner of his eye, he noticed something different. Something new.

"What's that?" he wondered. "Built into the door? That wasn't there before."

Being a curious sort, Elwood decided to investigate. He pushed on it with his tiny hands. To his surprise, it opened.

"Hm."

He stuck his nose in. And his head.

"Why, look at that."

He climbed in. It was no problem; no one climbs like a possum. A short fall, *Umph*!

Once inside, he looked around.

"Well, well. This is pretty darned nice. Why, I never imagined how nice it could be. And what's that, over there? A bunch of bananas? I looove bananas."

Chapter Eight

Old Sol peered over the horizon. He shone down upon God's creation with a cheery, auspicious glow. His rosy, ebullient cheeks seemed to make the misty dawn air sparkle with burgeoning enthusiasm. Another day.

A rooster greeted rosy Old Sol with a hearty, spirited cock-a-doodle-doo.

… A rooster greeted rosy Old Sol with a hearty, spirited, cock-a-doodle-doo!

… A rooster … … oh, never mind.

It was another day.

The alarm clock went off in the front bedroom of the old farmhouse. It clattered for only a second and abruptly ceased.

Then followed the words, loud enough that those at the barn and in the woods beyond might hear: "Beer-neese sauce! I'll smother that rooster in Beer-neese sauce!"

With those words, the farm, this genial, familial community at the end of the grassy lane, rustled to life.

Another day.

Star, the giant, useless but beautiful and graceful racehorse, and Okee Donkey – none of those things – stomped in their stalls.

Marv, who had overslept, scowled. Junior had left the downstairs TV on again last night.

Yes, the kid was back living with them, again. It was his mother, Mabel. She felt sorry for him. Marv couldn't figure it out. She was so tough and practical in every other endeavor. Nobody messed with the mockingbirds, and that was mostly thanks to Mabel. Not even the crows dared step within earshot. Even Emory, the hawk, kept his distance.

Marv had to laugh, recalling the time Emory actually tried to sneak into their nest while Mabel was off getting her nails done. Little did Emory know that she was only a shout away. That poor hawk. He was still trying to live that one down, getting thrashed and pummeled by an angry mama mockingbird. Marv could still remember the look on Emory's face when he turned and saw Mabel coming in low and fast and with all guns a'blazing.

"Ha! Priceless!"

Marv went downstairs and turned off the TV. Junior was laying there in the La-Z-Boy, with popcorn, jelly bellies, and candy wrappers scattered across his stomach and on the floor. He was snoring.

It was time to put his foot down. Marv knew it.

But there was the wife. She was a good wife. She meant well. She was just a bit of a pushover – sometimes.

Marv shook his head, grabbed his bowl of Cheepios, and went out to the veranda for a hurried breakfast.

He was late, so he gobbled them down.

"Darned Cock-a-doodle-done-did," he grumbled. "It's his job to get everyone up in the morning. I'm here for entertainment purposes only."

No use complaining, though. Marv wasn't one to complain, so he flew off to the top of the telephone pole and broke into a melodic, "Good morning to you; good morning to you; good morning, good morning, good morning to you –"

A lovely day. He glanced at the nest, home sweet home, in the bougainvillea bush. He shook his head.

"Danged yaps. Ya boot 'em out the one door, and they come right back in the other."

*   *   *

Pappy was finishing his Cheerios. A big day today.

First off, he had to check and see if they caught that dastardly armadillo in the new, improved trap.

"Poor Buddy," he said from behind the folds of his newspaper. "He can't stand livin' down there with that thing."

"Well, you are not killing it," Grandma announced. "You just keep trying. At some point, you'll outsmart her, or him. I have complete confidence that my husband is smarter than an armadillo."

"Can't say I'm so sure about that, Mammy," Pap said. "I've never seen anything like it. I think he, or she's, been jumpin' that barricade. How high can an armadilly jump, anyway?"

Kids and grandkids were getting up and around. The entire farm smelled like breakfast. There is nothing better: bacon, sausage, coffee, grits, biscuits, hash browns, the works. It was the standard, everyday breakfast around here – except for Pappy.

"You sure you don't want me to make you some eggs?"

No. Pappy was a busy man, a man with a lot on his mind. He had come up with a new plan overnight, just in case last night's didn't work. He had total confidence that it had, though; and that he would finally have that ornery, leprosy-carrying beast in his clutches.

Victory.

He got up, gave Grandma a kiss, grabbed a few pieces of bacon, stuffed them in his overalls pocket, and headed out the door. The screen door slammed behind him, and from across the pasture arose the blaring clamor of frenzied yapping and barking.

"Sheesh, that's annoying," Pappy mumbled. "Don't they ever stop?"

He whistled, which prompted more fireworks from the other side of the fence. He shook his head.

"Come ooon, BUDDY!" he shouted. Then he whistled again and sat down to put his boots on. A minute later, Buddy came running from somewhere, panting happily.

Buddy was definitely a morning person. Not all dogs are.

"So, how's it look, Buddy?" Pappy asked as he followed him around the corner, but brows and hearts deflated at the sight.

The trap was empty. No armadillo in sight.

Pappy and Buddy stared with consternation down the hole under the porch.

Hands set firmly on hips.

Both combatants wore deep, furrowed, contemplative scowls.

"Darned armadillies."

Yeah. Darned armadillies.

That afternoon

"What is going on around here?!" Grandma asked no one in particular.

"What?" Annie queried.

"Well, this time it's the cat. Look at this. She knows very well where the litter box is. I know this is called a mudroom, but ... really?" She looked around, and said, loudly in case Kitty was nearby, "You can't do this, Kitty! I don't know what's going on, but you better watch your step, little miss!"

"Maybe Kitty wants the litter box out here instead of in the closet," Annie suggested. "Maybe she has closet-o-mo, uh –"

"Claustrophobia," Grandma assisted. "That's when you're afraid of enclosed spaces."

"Right. Maybe Kitty has claus-tro-phobia."

"Great," Grandma sighed. "My cat has a phobia. Imagine that, having a phobia, living in this house. All right!" she said loudly, in case Kitty was nearby, "I'm moving the litter box out here, right where you took a ..." Grandma paused, glanced at Annie, "... right where you ... go!"

Annie giggled inside. Grandma almost said a bad word.

"And who's been leaving these stupid candy wrappers all over the place?!"

That evening

"Oh, look, everybody! It finally came!"

Everyone stood around the kitchen, engrossed as Grandma opened the much anticipated package. Ooos and ahhhs graced the air as she held up the Supersoaker for all to admire.

Pappy observed the proceedings from his throne: the kitchen chair.

"It looks like Excalibur," Uncle Randy noted.

Everyone agreed. It was magnificent. Shiny and colorful plastic, it seemed to radiate courage and fortitude.

Grandma agreed, by the looks of it, because she held it high over her head like Joan of Arc, and declared, "Squirrels, rapscallions, and all knaves beware!"

The people cheered.

It was evening. Lots of folks still were sitting around the kitchen, drinking coffee and soda and munching on chocolate fudge, with walnuts.

"So," Pappy said, "I suppose tomorrow is judgement day?"

Grandma looked askance – still in Joan of Arc, sword over the head, warrior pose – and declared, "So be it!"

The people cheered.

Pappy, meanwhile, looked to Buddy, and mumbled, "This has disaster written all over it."

You got that right, Buddy agreed.

"Well," Pappy suggested, "make sure someone tells Uncle Amos. He says he wants to be here to record the, uh, proceedings."

Pappy caught Davy's eye, and words were not necessary. Davy leaped to his feet and was out the door, Buddy at heel, off to the barn: Pappy's loyal, royal couriers.

He sat back on his throne. He nodded, non-committally. Tomorrow would be a day for the ages.

*   *   *

Meanwhile, next door, within the rusty ramparts and pooped-out palisades of The Grunge, plans were being discussed.

"That stupid cat probably already sounded the alarm," Lionel was complaining. "We're never gonna lure that kid over here now."

"But," Ernesto said, "we must try the plan we have. *Si?*"

"I suppose you're right," Lionel said. "You think? Uh … Vic?"

"Huh?" Vic was intently involved with an unattractive mole on his butt.

"Tomorrow's Saturday," Lionel said. "We should go ahead with the plan. You think?"

"Sure, I mean *ya'vol.*" He paused, deep in thought, and added, "Vhat plan?"

Everyone resisted rolling their eyes.

"The one Ernesto thought of? ... You know?"

"Uhhh."

"The one tomorrow morning? Out at the County Road?"

"Uhhh."

"The kid? Going wherever he goes on Saturday mornings?"

"Oh ... yeah," Vic replied, but without a whole lot of conviction. "The, uh –"

Sometimes it can be awful hard *not* to roll one's eyes.

Later

Pappy and Buddy were making their last foray into the outside night. The house was all buttoned up, everyone tucked away in bed but them. It was the last chance of the day to take in the moon, sky, stars, and the wonders of the nighttime world – and to go pee.

Small talk. Buddy time for Buddy and Pap.

"So, tomorrow's the big day," Pappy was saying. "Grandma versus those scurrilous squirrels. The showdown."

Yep. Don't want to miss that.

"I don't think anybody does. So," Pappy said, "Oke seems to be getting used to his latest trim."

He might be, but he still looks ridiculous.

"No doubt about that. Poor little guy. You know, the girls say he looks dashing."

I don't know if I'd call that dashing, Buddy mused.

They were just finishing up when Buddy noticed something out the corner of his eye.

"What do you see there, Buddy?" Pap asked.

Then he saw it, too.

"Now, how the heck did he, or she, get past that dad-blasted barricade?!"

Balls of fire flew from Pap's eyes. Buddy's as well.

This was becoming embarrassing.

Buddy looked to Pap, who looked around wildly. As one, their eyes locked on the big, plastic, five gallon bucket next to the hot bathtub.

"Don't let him, or her, get away, Buddy!"

Buddy went into action, making a dash around to cut him, or her, off – it was a standard flanking maneuver.

Pap had the bucket in hand and was moving fast – for an old man.

He was running and shouting, "Don't let him, or her, get away, Buddy!"

Oh, the little guy was fast, no doubt about that; but they strategically closed in, leaving no route of escape.

He, or she, tried one way, then the other.

Now! Buddy shouted. *Now, Pap! Now!*

Pappy made his move. Like greased lightning, he swooped in with the bucket and slammed it down, right over the ridiculous-looking creature from *Land Before Time*.

"GOT HIM! ... ... OR HER!"

Then came hesitation. Disbelief. How could this be? It was too easy.

Buddy and Pap looked at each other, and their victory came home to them. Surprise turned to smiles and grins, then whoops of joy and guffaws of glory. Together, they joined hands and – without taking pressure from the bucket – they danced and frolicked around it with shouts of jubilation and ultimate, happy-feet triumph.

Following the brief, but effusive, celebration, Pappy said, "All right, Buddy. We gotta be real careful turnin' this thing right side up. The critical moment is after it's up, but before we can slide the lid under it. The trick is to use a scooping motion."

A scooping motion, Buddy repeated. *Got it. I'm ready when you are.*

"Okay," Pap said. The stress, the enormity, of the moment showed in his wizened eyes. "I'll count to three, right?"

Right.

"Ready?"

Ready.

"Okay. One ... two –"

All of a sudden, there came a strange sound from inside the bucket, as if they had captured a tiny tornado.

They looked at it curiously.

"What the hec –" And before the "k" could exit Pappy's mouth, there came a loud crunching sound, and the side of the bucket blew to pieces just as a blurry whirlwind zipped right under Pap's legs and darted off into the night.

Man and Dog stared after it a while, long after it disappeared into the orange grove. Both wore dumbfounded, and dumb-looking, expressions.

After a time, Pappy said, "Did you see that?"

I think so.

"But ... that's impossible! It's a brand new bucket! I'd be hard-pressed ta put a hammer through that thing!"

Buddy could only shrug.

They stared a moment more.

Then Buddy scratched his chin, and said, *Um, is there any way we could pour a concrete wall between me and him, or her? You know? Under the porch?*

Pappy thought a minute, then mumbled, "It'd have to be a pretty thick wall."

Yeah, Buddy agreed. *The thicker the better.*

"Yeah."

Yeah.

Later still

Life had never been better.

Elwood could get used to this. As a matter of fact, he already had.

He had a routine even, which mostly entailed sleeping and eating.

That's right. Living here, in the house, there was no need to spend time foraging. Nope. Here, it was all laid out before him, like a banquet. A feast!

Not only that, he could eat at his leisure these days, and it was some of the best food he'd ever had. There was plenty of fresh fruit, and vegetables – no sense in getting out of shape – but there was also the cookie jar and the candy jar and the peanut brittle jar. That was not to mention the under-the-sink garbage, which could be astonishingly fruitful, so to speak.

He noticed his pants were getting a little tight these days. He had, by now, permanently undone the top button.

Elwood yawned grandly, exposing a mouthful of sharp, white teeth. He rolled over, smacked his thin lips, and peered out the end of his box, which was located on the top shelf of the broom closet and labeled "Vacuum Cleaner Bags." He wondered what time it was. It was hard to tell in here. From the sounds of the house, though, it was time to get up and get to work. The kitchen was right around the corner.

He climbed down from his apartment and took a good, long stretch and yawn.

Wake up, Elwood. He told himself. *You have to keep an eye out for that cat.*

That had been his biggest worry, moving into the house: the cat. But, as it turned out, she was out most of every night doing whatever it was that cats did. Yep, it had really worked out well. Sometimes, Pappy would walk in unannounced, coming down to raid the refrigerator in the middle of the night. It was clear, though, that he was half blind in the dark, not to mention he was a really messy snack maker – always a good thing.

And the butter dish. *Oh, my gosh! The butter dish!* Elwood had never imagined anything as wondrous as a butter dish. He was always sure to put the lid back on when he finished. He wasn't exactly a neat freak, but for Elwood it was a practical matter. Nobody wants flies in their butter.

He pushed the bifold door back and looked around.

The coast was clear.

But ... what's that?

Elwood approached the object placed in the corner of the mudroom. He sniffed, checking it out.

Hm. That's nice ... and convenient. A bathroom, just for me.

Chapter Nine

Old Sol peered over the horizon. He shone down upon God's creation with a cheery, auspicious glow. His rosy, ebullient cheeks seemed to make the misty dawn air sparkle with ... ... never mind. It was another day.

Kitty strutted into the house, tail up, nose held high. It had been a good night: death to rats! Mice as well. She thought she might be coming down with something, though. She tried to dismiss the disturbing possibilities of cooties or leprosy, but it was hard. She got a shiver every time she recalled crawling through that cootie hole.

Grandma said her good mornings.

"Meow."

She was the only one up.

"Meow."

Scratches, pleasant conversation, then the main event: breakfast.

Into the mudroom they went, Kitty's tail lighting the way, so to speak.

Grandma was getting the food ready when her demeanor suddenly changed.

"Now, look here, Kitty. I am *very* disappointed in you lately. The past few mornings I've been getting up to a mess on the floor in here."

Huh? Kitty didn't know what she was talking about.

"Anyway, I put your litter box in the corner over there –"

What?

"– because you can't seem to find it anymore."

Huh?

"I better not have to clean up after you anymore, understand? And if you can't use the litter box, like you're supposed to, I'll have no choice but to lock you out of the house."

What?!

Kitty frowned as Grandma set the bowl down and left.

She picked at her food and looked around suspiciously.

"Somethin's goin' on around here," Kitty mumbled to herself. "And I don't like it; not one bit. I wonder if it's those squirrels that have her rattled. Hm. Maybe I should take out a few of 'em myself. I'll rip their little heads off, help Grandma out a little."

*   *   *

Grandma did not need any help, armed as she was with the SS-550 Max Magnablaster Double-fire Supersoaker II.

Everyone had gathered in the kitchen after breakfast. Even Uncle Amos was there with his cameras: still-shot and video. It was his hobby, recording all the goings on at the farm. He called himself the Chronicler-in-Chief. Everyone else called him Uncle Amos.

So far, there had been no action. It was as if the enemy knew something was up.

Cousin Denny gave up waiting and left for work. There had been a couple more defections as the stake-out dragged on.

"Ambush takes patience!" Grandma had declared as one after the other slipped out.

"I'll wait for the movie," Aunt Janice said upon her departure.

It did seem anti-climactic. At first, Grandma had been at the ready, like a sniper on a rooftop. Then she did some dishes while she waited; she started a bunt cake.

"Hey, look!" from some cousin or aunt or uncle. "Here comes one now!"

Like a well-trained U.S. Navy Seal, Grandma snatched up her weapon. She checked the load and set the magazine to double-concussion-fire. She flipped the safety.

Determination welled in her eyes.

The rapt audience gathered around. Camera lenses focused, ready to roll, and –

"Action!"

*   *   *

The lone soldier, a forward scout, tested the field of battle, which was still damp with morning mist. Cautiously, and with senses attuned, he made his way deep into enemy territory, beyond the flower garden with the bird bath and lamppost to the croton bushes.

He paused, taking in the situation. He could make them out, the enemy forces, aligned against him as they were, observing his every movement from inside the kitchen window. There *she* was: their leader, their general, their commander-in-chief, looking down at him from her lofty palisade. It appeared they had developed some new, innovative, state-of-the-art weapon.

Lieutenant Artie, the lone, undeterred soul, glanced back at the tree, to all the watching squirrel eyes. They were counting on him.

"Well, it's now or never," he mumbled to himself, and he scampered onto the porch rail – a most vulnerable position. He would have to move quickly.

And he did. He leaped out, up, and onto the birdfeeder. Without delay, he started swinging it, spinning it wildly so seed and grain would spill and fly out. As he worked, he kept an eye on the window. He could see them in there. It looked like the entire forces of the army, navy, and marines had gathered, and all eyes were on him.

What was that in Grandma's hands? Artie wondered. It looked like a squirt gun, but a whole lot bigger.

Whatever it was, she was braced with it, in firing position, and taking aim.

Artie could not imagine what was about to befall him as he toiled and spun, tossing seeds and grain to the ground, bounty for his people – or squirrels.

*   *   *

Inside the kitchen, no one moved a muscle. You could have heard a pin drop. A dozen faces stared out the window as the lone squirrel defied Grandma's warnings and made a full-on, bold-faced assault on the birdfeeder.

No one uttered a word. Grandma concentrated on the swinging target, her finger poised on the trigger.

Easy. Easy. FIRE!!

No one had ever witnessed anything like it: the raw, air-quaking power of two photon-torpedo-grade blasts of water careening across the yard and wiping out everything in their path.

Double *KA-PHLOOSH!!!*

There was a moment of silence afterward, as all looked on in wonder – and victory. And horror? Yes, there seemed to be nothing left of the squirrel.

"No, look!" Davy shouted. "It's way over there, almost to the tree!"

No one could believe the power of the SS-550 Max Magnablaster Double-fire Supersoaker II.

The soggy tuft of fur lay there, unmoving.

Everyone looked to Grandma, who turned white. Her lower lip trembled. The dread weapon tumbled from her grasp, clunking bitterly into the sink.

"Oh," she gasped, holding onto the sink for support. "What have I done? What have I done?!"

Loved ones gathered around, comforting her with gentle hands, but there could be no solace.

"Wait!" Cousin Missy exclaimed. "Look! It's moving. It's moving!"

All eyes went to the drenched ball of fur.

The little guy raised his head. He looked around, then towards the open kitchen window. With fear radiating from his eyes, he desperately tried to get away, but he couldn't. It appeared his back legs wouldn't work.

"No!!" Grandma cried, clutching her hands to her chest.

Then they all watched, yes, in horror, as the little fellow dragged himself towards the tree, an inch at a time.

"No!!" Grandma pleaded. "No! No!! No!!!"

But there was nothing they could do, nothing but watch as other squirrels came down the tree to see how their little friend was.

"Why?! Why?!!" Grandma cried to the heavens. Then she glanced sideways, at Uncle Amos, who was avidly chronicling, zooming in on the struggling creature with his telephoto lens.

Her eyes narrowed.

"CUT! CUT!! STOP FILMING!!!"

*   *   *

Across the way, Artie was pretty shaken. He hadn't seen it coming. He was addled, for sure; but not so much that he hadn't the capacity for good humor and a little bit of stick-it-to-her-itiveness.

As he dragged himself towards the tree, and noticed all the concerned squirrel faces, he winked at them and gave them the "O-kay," sign, indicating that he was faking it. By the looks of it – with Grandma wailing and moaning and carrying on in the kitchen window – it was working.

Yep, the oldest trick in the book: the guilt trip – the greatest weapon of all.

No, Artie did not think he'd have to worry about the SS-550 Max Magnablaster Double-fire Supersoaker II anymore after today.

Chapter Ten

Saturday morning was piano lesson day for Davy.

He liked playing piano, and he liked Mrs. Benderhoven, his piano teacher, as well. She was beautiful, and smart, and smelled real good sitting right next to him on that piano bench.

It wasn't that far, by bicycle, just three miles or so, on the outskirts of town.

He was sure to latch the gate. Then he was off, down the hardly ever used County Road, getting up a nice speed. Davy liked to go fast.

Zoom.

Something caught his eye, though, something that made him slow down, then hit the brakes.

"Aw," he said, "poor thing," and he pulled off the road.

It was the chihuahua from next door, the three-legged one.

"Aww."

Grandma said Davy had a big heart, and it was true.

Something had happened to the dog. It was dragging itself towards the neighbor's gate.

"Are you okay, little fellow?" Davy asked.

The dog whimpered and continued dragging itself, piteously and in an agony-filled way, towards the gate.

Davy lay his bicycle down and hurried over to help.

*   *   *

Five sets of eyes observed from the bushes along the County Road fence.

"It's working!" Ali shouted, in a whisper.

"Bloimy!" Cornwall exclaimed. "That bloody chihuahua is doynamoite! Whoiy, 'e's gonna bloody do it, 'e is!"

They were all lined up on their haunches, ready to pounce.

"I can't believe it!" Lionel said, sinisterly rubbing his paws together. "This was a great idea Ernesto had. Isn't it? ... Vic?"

"*Ya'vol*," Vic said, his eyes focused on the kid. "I cannot vait to tear zhat high-minded, pink-fleshed kid limb from bloody limb."

Lionel looked to the others.

"Um … I, uh, I don't know if that's in the plan, Vic. Tearing cats to bits is one thing; I mean, we just want to put a scare into those lousy Last Resorters so they keep that stupid cat off our property." He paused. "You know? … Vic?"

Vic's eyes were fixed on the kid, now inching closer to Ernesto, now almost to the gate.

"Ve shall see about zhat," Vic mumbled under his breath.

"Um … really, Vic," Lionel gaped at the others. "We'll be in some pretty hot water with Old Man Perkins if we tear the kid limb from limb. Society looks down on that. You know? … Vic?"

Vic glared at Lionel. His teeth started to resemble a horseshoe, and a guttural growl rumbled from deep in his belly.

They could hear the kid talking, coaxing Ernesto, who was putting on an utterly fabulous show, by the way. He really looked like he'd been run over or something, whining, whimpering, gasping for air, and dragging himself up the shellrock driveway.

"Come on, little fellow," the kid said. "I won't hurt you. Let me help you."

Lionel glanced at Vic, who was drooling with excitement, his lower jaw quivering with visceral, animal meltdown.

"Ve vait for my signal," Vic said, his voice low and menacing, possibly deranged with spite and hatred.

Ernesto was to the gate. He was crawling under. He signaled, thumbs up, to those waiting in the bushes.

The kid was following still; he was right behind.

The gate squeaked as it opened.

Vic and the others were rigid on their haunches, ready to spring into action.

The moment was here. The kid was right there. Viper could not contain herself any longer, though.

"Arf! Arf! Ar –"

Lionel grabbed her by the snout. "SHH!!"

Everyone froze.

"Is someone over there?" the kid asked, his hand still on the gate. "In those bushes?"

Lionel looked to Vic. His eyes were wild. His teeth bared.

"Ve attack now," he said, and he took a deep breath to give the command.

Lionel, his eyes wide, was about to respond, except there arose a loud *BEEEEEEEP!* Everyone looked to see a truck pulling into the drive.

"It's the boss!" Lionel cried.

"The boss!" everyone repeated.

They looked at each other and got down off their haunches.

"Bloimy," Cornwall said. "That'll do it for me. Oi'm 'eadin' back to the bloody 'ouse, Oi am." And off he went.

Ernesto was back on his three legs, looking confused and a little nervous. He glanced between the boss and the gang.

"Hey, you! Kid!" came a familiar voice from the cab of the truck. "You git th' hell off'n my prope'ty! And don't ye never come back! Ye hea?!"

The kid closed the gate and tried to explain what he had been doing, but only for a second. Then he dashed for his bicycle and sped off.

"Dang it!" Lionel grumbled. He glared at Viper. "You just couldn't keep your mouth shut, could you?"

Viper shrugged, folded her arms, and replied, "Maybe it's a good thing. Otherwise, the old man would have got here right when we were tearing that kid limb from limb." She looked to Vic for support.

Vic frowned. "*Ya'vol.* Perhaps it vas gudt zhat der little shih could not keep her big mouth shut. *Ya?*"

"Hmph," Lionel grumbled.

They all waited for Old Man Perkins to get the truck through the gate so they could act like they were happy he was home, barking, howling, and carrying on like a bunch of purebred nutballs.

*　　　*　　　*

Oke was like most donkeys: conceited. Not a lot; maybe conceited is too strong a term. Regardless, he was proud to be a donkey. Donkeys, throughout history, have been the most useful animal to humans. It's arguably inarguable, based on the evidence.

There are few that can truly compete for the title of "most useful to civilization."

Dogs might come to mind right away, but how much did they really do to advance civilization?

Have you seen how much they can carry on their backs? It's embarrassing.

Oh, sure. They make great companions, and are small enough to curl up at your feet in a warm, comfortable bed on a cold night. Sure. They also offer great protection with those sharp, canine teeth; but, again –

Have you seen how much they can carry on their backs?

Primitive peoples all over the world had dogs do many things, yes, but civilizations? Civilizations are constructed not from comfortable sleep partners and sharp, shiny teeth, but the ability to move things. Dogs, for all their noble qualities, cannot move things in any quantity.

Donkeys. That is how it was done.

Oh. Horses? Really? Sure, they run fast and look good and can even carry a lot, but how far?

Not very.

And how much do horses need to eat?

A LOT!!

Then, of course, there's the "skittish" thing. Horses jump at the slightest noise or sudden movement. Their first reflex is to run away.

Really? Run away?

Donkeys cannot fathom such an act. They simply do *not* run away. In fact, the donkey's first reflex is to stand and fight.

Why do you think they call it kicking ... ass?

It would never enter Oke's mind, or any donkey's mind, to shy away from a fight.

Oke had once "killed" a coyote that had invaded his pasture. It was in the papers and everything. The only one who knew that the coyote had actually run into a tree and broken his own neck was Oke, and he wasn't talking. The fact was, however, Oke had been chasing the coyote, and he would have kicked his butt if the stupid thing had not run right into that tree – the only one, by the way, all by itself, out in the middle of the pasture.

These talents, Oke's pugilistic skills, bring us back to dogs, and their contribution to humanity and civilization – that is, their protective and fighting abilities. This is all well and true, but fact is, donkeys can kick dogs' "asses." Maybe not every donkey versus every dog; but in balance –

Donkeys would stomp those scrawny, shiny-toothed upstarts into the dust.

That was Oke's standard argument in the matter, anyway.

But it was good. It *is* good to be proud of who you are. Oke was proud to be a donkey. And no one knew more ass jokes, by the way, than Okee Donkey, except for possibly a proctologist. *Ha!* Regardless, this inner pride, instilled in him from thousands of years of countless forebears, made Oke, as many donkeys are, a tad vain about his appearance. Which, at the moment, was less than stellar, ever since Grandma had shown up with her shears the other day – and wearing a wicked, Butcher of Lyon grin on her face.

In general, Grandma was Oke's favorite person on earth. She was good and pure and always fed him on time. But there was a streak of evil inside her, obviously, or she would not subject him, Oke, a donkey she claimed to love, to such base, unseemly humiliation.

After the deed was done, she and all the girls and kids would stand around and laugh at him and say things like: "Oh, he looks so cute! Tee hee!" and "Oh, he's so handsome! Tee hee!" or "Oh, aren't you nice and cool now, Oke?"

No. I was fine before, the way God made me. How about I shave all your heads? You'll be so cute! And handsome! And nice and cool!

It can be tough, being a donkey. But Oke was as tough as they came.

And, at the moment, about as humiliated as well.

He was out in the pasture, minding his own business, munching on some Bermuda grass, when he heard it.

He rolled his eyes. Big sigh.

Oke had avoided this part of the pasture lately just because of this. But it was the only place with Bermuda growing in lush, juicy profusion.

He mumbled under his breath, "Doofuses."

There was a slight rise on the other side of the fence, so the Sinister Six were looking down on him.

"Oh, lookee, lookee, comrades!" It was the big, stupid one. "Old Fat Ass vas been run ofer by der lawnmower!"

Oh, that is so funny.

Oke ignored them.

"Hey, baldy!" one of them shouted. "What do you call a group of rabbits hopping backwards?! ... A receding hairline!"

Oke pretended they weren't there.

"'Ey, cue ball! Can Oi rub your 'ead for me fortune?! Oi needs ta know what's for bloody dinner t'noight!"

It was starting to get to Oke, though.

"Hey, Meester Fat Ass! What do you call a barber that only works on bald people?"

Oh, please, no.

"He ees called a *air* styleest. Geet eet? *Air* styleest?!"

Another good thing about donkeys is their ability to take a beating and keep on going, but this was quite a pummeling. Quite a pummeling indeed.

Oke glanced at them, just on the other side of the fence, behaving like lunatics. His blood boiled.

Just ignore them. Enjoy your Bermuda.

"Hey, fellas!" the beagle shouted. "How's about we call old lard butt Glassy Assy from now on!"

It was getting ever more difficult for Oke to enjoy his Bermuda.

"Yeah! Glassy Assy!"

"*Ya'vol*! Gudt von! Glassy Assy! Hey! Glassy Assy! You look like der big glass ass zhing!"

Oh, how Oke hated them.

But what could he do?

It has been argued by wise men for ages past: Why does the donkey stay inside the fence when, clearly, he can get out any time he wants?

The answer brings us back to dogs. Dogs are loyal, yes. But donkeys are loyal, too. Maybe not *as* loyal, but loyal just the same. Regardless, donkeys stay put because they choose to. Possibly, too, because it's not so bad a gig, free food and lodging, an occasional brushing, and nothing to do all day but graze – and look good.

Which Oke did not; at least not at the moment, not with this ludicrous haircut he was sporting.

The dogs continued to cackle deliriously and carry on like a pack of deranged banshees.

Donkeys do not handle humiliation well.

He had no doubt he could take one or two out; that fat English hound for sure; the little ones would be hard to pin down.

Finally, Oke lifted his oversized head. He studied them.

"Vhy, just look at him!" the German said. "He is staring us down! Oh, look at how brafe he must be!"

"Yeah!" the others shouted with glee. "Brave Glassy Assy! Brave Glassy Assy!"

It was almost too much.

No. By this point, it *was* too much.

The fury of thousands of years of being made fun of by dogs and horses and even mules boiled to the surface, and Oke charged the fence, the fence post his objective. With masterful precision, he turned ass-to, and *WHAP!!*

Gone.

Quickly, to the next one. *WHAP!!*

And the next one.

WHAP!!

The dogs were in a frenzy until the dawn of realization: "I theek that donkey ees coming through!"

Which would not be necessary, at least not today, for there they went, all of them, tails between their legs, over the rise.

Oke snorted and stomped and considered giving chase, but he figured he was in enough trouble with wrecking the fence. There would be a big to-do if he hunted them down and stomped them into the dust one at a time.

Plus, there was Old Man Perkins and his shotgun.

No. Oke thought he'd made his point.

Buddy ran up. Star did as well – after Buddy had arrived and the coast was clear.

"What happened?" Buddy asked.

"Oh," Oke sighed. "Just had to give those doofuses from next door a warning shot over the bow."

Buddy studied the busted and broken fence with a contemplative brow.

"They, uh, they mentioned the uh, haircut … didn't they?"

"Hmph." Oke grunted. "I don't want to talk about it right now."

"No prob," Buddy said. "I'll tell Pap it wasn't your fault. They drove you to it."

"You can say that again," Oke mumbled. "Doofuses."

*   *   *

Cats can be obdurate, stubborn, yes, and even mule-headed. Curious as well, as we have all heard. Yet where does curiosity get cats?

Kitty was leaning against the corner of the playhouse, loitering and appearing to smoke a cigarette while keeping an eye on those impertinent mockingbirds. Of all the birds in all of birddom, from Kitty's experience, the mockingbird variety was the most irritating.

It wasn't just the constant singing, the bursting out in delirial song and dance for no apparent reason, the never-ending emanations of bucolic joy and pastoral delight until Kitty's head was about to explode. No. It was more than that.

In a word, it came down to attitude. Mockingbirds, from Kitty's experience, were the only birds that exhibited no fear of cats; and to a cat that is very important, especially with something so low and feathery and flitty as a bird. Why, even Emory, the hawk, showed the proper respect when Kitty was around.

"Doity, stinkin' mockin'birds," Kitty mumbled to herself.

She had her eye on the young one, Junior. Kitty thought he would have moved on by now. There would be another brood on the way soon.

Junior, Kitty noticed, was not at all like his parents. He was rash and careless, reckless even. Why, just the other day Kitty was over on the porch – in the middle of her afternoon roll, nap, and bask in cat glory – when she opened her eyes to see that stupid kid, right there, perched on the porch rail. There he was, just staring down at her with a stupid, smug, disrespectful look glued to his face.

Oh, she could have done it. Kitty was quite the lunger. He was right there: a hearty helping of mockingbird pie. But it had been a bad time with Grandma nearby playing Go Fish with the twins. Grandma, for some reason, was not impressed with Kitty's cruel, psychopathic, and murderous skills.

He was up there now, on the telephone line, taunting her. Pesky kid.

In close quarters, Kitty would be master of such a feathery waif, but out in the open it was a different story. Kitty had heard that the men who flew the airplanes in dogfights during the war had learned their craft from observing mockingbirds. It was just one more reason to loathe them – mockingbirds.

This insolent kid was starting to aggravate Kitty. He should have moved out weeks ago.

Punk.

She wasn't afraid of him, of course, but it can be startling when you're all of a sudden being dive-bombed from out of nowhere, and for no reason at all. Kitty was accustomed to constant harassment whenever Marv and Mabel had little ones around; it was their job to protect them. But this kid? He just did it for fun.

Oh, nothing made Kitty angrier than when that kid would swoop down out of nowhere and scare the unholy bejabbers out of her, then fly off laughing.

Kitty appeared to take a long drag from a cigarette, like an old time gangster under a streetlamp on a dark, misty night.

She had a lot on her mind lately.

For one thing, something was going on in that house. She was certain someone had been using her bathroom. She wondered if it was one of the twins.

Mostly, what raged in Kitty's mind, these days, was those mo-rons from next door.

It irked her. She had run for her life. She might not have escaped at all if not for that hideous, disease-infested thing that lived under the porch. It was embarrassing. Word was getting around, all over the forest and the other farms along the County Road, that Kitty had been rescued by an, ugh, armadillo.

She wondered what was going on with their plan to kidnap Davy. Probably just talk, she figured. In that regard, Kitty remained torn over whether to tell Buddy what she had heard.

She could hear it now, Pappy declaring to all who passed through, "Yep! This here's the best watchcat ever!"

Ugh.

Kitty was curious. She could not help but wonder at what was going on over there with those whacked out nutballs. She gazed across the pasture, towards the neighbor's property. Okee Donkey was out there at the far corner, grazing, and who should show up but the Loudmouthed Nutball Club.

She couldn't catch all of it, but they were obviously making fun of him over his new haircut. Kitty had to agree, it looked preposterous, as always. She didn't say anything about it to Oke. She didn't say much to him or Star at all, actually. They were stock animals. Kitty did not fraternize with stock animals. It simply was not becoming, for a cat.

They got along fine, though. Oke and Star were in full understanding that Kitty was the one who kept their barn clear of rodents. And Bundy Mac, of course; the rat snake – credit where credit due. Now there was someone Kitty had no desire to associate with, Bundy Mac. But then, Kitty was a cat. She didn't really associate with anyone, unless there was a morsel or a friendly – convenient – scratch involved.

She wasn't really paying attention to the Nutball Club, but she could tell by Oke's ears and other body language that he was growing upset. Kitty had seen what

Oke could do. There was the unfortunate rattlesnake that got into the pasture that time – very messy. Of course, there was also the unlucky coyote who strayed in there; not to mention that time someone forgot to let Oke out of his stall on time.

Kitty took interest. She leaned back and got comfortable and had another cigarette.

All of a sudden, all Donkey broke loose. No. Literally. Oke was on a rampage.

Kitty sat up.

Now, this is entertainment!

Kitty, not one to be impressed with anyone or anything but herself, was.

My gosh! Look at him go!

She looked around to see if anyone else was watching. It was one fence post after another: *Cr-rack! Cr-rack! Cr-rack!*

She looked at Buddy, up on the porch, sleeping.

Darn it! Wake up! Look! LOOK!!

But Buddy just lay there.

Kitty was beside herself, glancing between the riot at the fence-line and Buddy. He was sound asleep.

Finally, Kitty couldn't take it any longer, and she shouted, "ME-YOOOOW!!!"

Buddy woke up. In an instant, he was off the porch and on his way to the rescue.

As he ran past, he shouted, "Good job, Kitty!"

Kitty cringed, chagrined – *I am not a watchcat!*

Yet she was also enamored with the possibility that this could be the day. Yes, this could be the day that Buddy and Oke would break through enemy lines and crush and destroy that unmannerly pestilence from next door.

Except Oke stopped at the border. He bucked and raged and snorted warnings to the rascally cowards, who were dashing off into the woods with tails between their legs. Oke, however, did not pursue.

Kitty was in a tizzy.

"Go! GO!" she shouted, encouraging him onward. To no avail.

With a sigh, Kitty watched as Buddy arrived. She hoped his presence would spur Oke forward. But, no. They just stood there, watching.

"Great," Kitty grumbled. "Just like Lee at Gettysburg."

Once it was clear that there would be no more action, Kitty got up from her comfortable position and headed across the yard for the house, a casual, unhurried stroll. But then, all of a sudden, from out of nowhere came a dive-bombing, juvenile delinquent, scaring the unholy bejabbers out of her.

"Curse you!" Kitty railed, shaking her fist at Junior as he flew off, laughing up a storm.

Staring after him, she mumbled, "Oh, you's goin' down, ya pesky punk."

Chapter Eleven

Pappy was late – getting into his hot bathtub, that is.

There were several reasons for his tardiness, including trouble getting the fire under it started. Mostly, however, it was because he had spent much of the afternoon fixing the fence Oke tore down. There had been some choice words for Oke that afternoon.

Grandma was across the turnout, saying, "Heeere, chicke-chicke-chicke-chicke-chickee-chickee-chickee." She was putting the chickens, the girls she called them, to bed – back into their coop for the night.

Pappy hid behind the mother-in-law tongues, checked to make sure no one was looking, then he shed skivs and scampered into the hot bathtub.

Ahhhh.

He could hear Grandma over there. She couldn't find Matilda.

"Heeere, Tilly-willy-willy-willy-willy-willy-willy!"

He smiled, and mumbled, "Darned good woman."

It was good. It was very good, after a long, arduous day, just to sit back in his hot bathtub.

"Hey, Buddy!" he shouted towards the under-the-porch. "Come on over!"

Pappy frowned.

"Hmph," he grumbled. He picked up his clipboard. "Let's see. What happens next? Oh, yeah. Big Tommy has taken off with little Bertie, and Bo has to go after him."

Pappy scribbled studiously at his clipboard, occasionally looking off into space, sometimes grimacing and feverishly erasing. He paused for a refreshing drink of beer and noticed a tiny spider had made his home on his shoulder.

"You're lucky I'm a benevolent ruler," Pappy mumbled. Gently but deftly, he flicked the little guy off; but, unfortunately, he went right into the water. No problem. Pap nudged him over to the edge of the tub, where the spider climbed to safety. "Now, off you go," Pap said with a satisfied smile.

He was about to get back to his clipboard, except out of nowhere Big Boy, the oversized anole, appeared and gobbled up the tiny fellow.

Pap was appalled.

"Really?" he said. "You're not fat enough already? Ya gotta eat my personal friends now?"

Big Boy did some pushups and dashed off, back into his forest of mother-in-law tongues.

"Hey! Buddy!" Pappy shouted. "You're missin' everything over here!"

*   *   *

"I doubt it," Buddy grumbled.

Buddy was busy. He had no time for Pappy's little dramas.

He had work to do, repairing and reinforcing the hole that that durntestable cootie-carrier had dug through his impervious wall. This time, he had packed the sand extra firm by sitting down on it over and over, real hard.

"Hey, Buddy! Come on!"

Buddy was just finishing up. Finally, he was safe from insidious, festering disease once again. He took one last look around, sighed, and headed out from his under-the-porch.

Whoa! It's later than I thought.

He took a good look around. Grandma and the kids were out at the barn, calling the girls in.

Well, let's go see what's up with Pap.

He ambled on over.

Pap was fully involved in his clipboard. When Pap was fully involved, Buddy could do a Turkish jig in a chartreuse tutu, and Pap would not notice.

What's up, Paperino?

"Oh, hey, Buddy. Just chillin' while I'm hot'n. So, how's the new, improved, impenetrable barrier comin'?"

I think it's pretty good. I packed it real hard this time. I put my butt into it, like you said.

"Good idea." Pappy doled out a dollop of beer. "Danged armadilly."

Yeah. Danged armadilly. And thanks.

"No prob. So, ya say his name is Harlan?"

That's what he said, but at the time I just wanted out of there. You know what I'm saying?

"Oh, I know what you're sayin'. So, I think Harlan is a boy's name. Right?"

I think so, but wasn't there an actress named Harley something? Couldn't Harley be short for Harlan?

"Who knows?" Pappy mumbled.

So, Pap, Buddy said. *You shouldn't hold it against Oke for busting the fence into a thousand pieces today. He was under a lot of pressure, with those numbskulls from next door making fun of his new haircut.*

"Eh," Pap shrugged. "I'm already over it. Danged donkey."

Yeah. Danged donkey.

"Oh, my gosh!" Pappy suddenly exclaimed, horror in his voice. "Look at this! Just look at it!"

Buddy looked.

"It's those dag-nabbed amorous anoles again!" Pap shouted, waving his hand. "Cut it out, Big Boy! I told you! Ya gotta do that somewhere else! Go on with your little ... whoever she is!" He splashed water on them. "Somewhere else! Somewhere else, I command!"

*   *   *

"Oh, look!" Annie exclaimed. "Pappy's chasing amorous anoles away from his hot bathtub again!"

The women and girls were all gathered in the after-dinner-cleaned-up kitchen. They had all seen it before.

Grandma, meanwhile, was teetering on despondent. Frayed nerves rattled her every thought. She was cleaning things that did not need cleaning.

"Why don't you sit down, Mom?"

And, "Why don't you sit down, Grandma?"

It had gone on all day. It was what she did when she was distraught, and this was as distraught as it got. She put up a good front, though. At least she tried.

But the kids could tell.

She looked out the kitchen window, at the tree beyond. They had gone out and searched for him, the ... the victim. Or the ... body. But there had been none.

She and the kids had all looked upward, into the expansive canopy, at the squirrels chattering down at them.

Grandma had listened to them, and she knew what they were saying.

*   *   *

"And did you see the look on her face when she said, 'Are you up there, little guy? If you are, I'm ... I'm so sorry!'"

Artie howled. Everyone else did as well. All of them were having a merry, festive time. The old oak shook with the natty rhythm of good humor and wholehearted hilarity.

"Then she started crying!" Peto shouted. "Oh, boo-hoo!"

"Ha, ha, ha, ha, ha!" Everyone laughed, having a big old time of it.

Everyone except for old Chuck.

He scowled. He peered over his reading glasses. He took them off, and everyone settled down. He looked off in the distance, pensively.

72

"It was very funny, yes," he said. "And we are fortunate that Artie here was not seriously injured. I must say, it was a stroke of genius on his part to think of utilizing the guilt trip and then pulling it off so well. Congratulations, Artie."

The Darwins and their kin, and even other denizens of the tree, cheered.

"It is true," Chuck continued. "No one falls for the guilt trip like humans do. But we must remember the empathy that Grandma displayed today. It was thoroughly amusing, I must admit, but it should not be dismissed lightly: her sense of compassion, her humanity; just as we should not lose sight of our own squirrelmanity. We must be aware of motivations, others' motivations. And hers, Grandma's, can be, we all must admit, generous – to a fault even. It is true, she does give the birds more feed than us, but she does consider us when she sets some out at the bottom of our tree, which is more than a lot of people would do."

There was a mumbling. A grumbling even.

"What are you saying?" Chloe asked. "That we shouldn't knock over her birdfeeder anymore?"

There was a collective gasp, followed by more grumblings.

Chuck looked to Mrs. Darwin – Grandma Darwin. Then he sighed heavily and looked off in the distance.

"No." He returned his gaze to his clan. "I am not saying that. It is part of our makeup to spill everything from the birdfeeder as messily and as efficiently as we can, but … but we can show some level of restraint. Can we not? What I am saying is that we should not take more than we need. We should all live within our own means; that is, what we can actually consume at any given time. It is a waste, and even a crime against nature and God, to do otherwise."

A murmur passed like a breeze through wide, sweeping branches of the stately old oak tree.

"Artie?" Chuck said, and everyone's eyes went to the bold, precocious, popular young firebrand. "What say you?"

Artie Darwin looked around at the others. He scowled, and nodded – though cryptically.

*　　　*　　　*

Later on, as it was getting late, Pappy and Grandma were watching TV.

"Don't worry about it, cuddly-poo," Pappy was saying. "It was an accident. How was anyone to know that thing was comparable to a double barrel bazooka? Anyway, I think the squirrel was fine. I mean, how else did he get back up the tree?"

"Or," Grandma sighed, "maybe he dragged himself off, into the orange grove. I hear that's how they do it. They send the old and injured off to die by themselves."

73

Pap grimaced. "I don't know, munchikins. I think that's Indians you're thinking of. Indians used to do that, not squirrels. I'm tellin' ya, he was just knocked for a loop is all. He's fine. The little guy'll be back at it tomorrow, knockin' that feeder loopy and spillin' every bit of feed to the ground."

"Really?" Grandma said, hope in her voice. She wiped at a tear. "You think so?"

"Oh, absolutely," Pappy said. "Right, Buddy?"

Buddy lifted his head. He flopped it back down.

"I hope so," Grandma sighed. "I feel just awful."

"That's because you have a good heart," Pappy said. "People with good hearts always feel worse than the rest of us."

Grandma couldn't help but smile.

A little while later, Pappy and Buddy were telling her all about their newest plan of attack against the armadillo. Grandma was listening, but she was a little distracted.

"Hey, Mammy," Pappy asked. "Is Harley, the girl's name, short for Harlan?"

"I don't know. Why?"

"Oh … no reason."

They went on and on, discussing various strategies and tactics, what they would be doing the next day after this newest, latest, highest-walled, most-improved trap system failed.

"You know, I was thinking," Grandma said.

Buddy and Pap took interest.

"About your predicament," she added.

"Yes?"

"Well, I was thinking. You said he's a real digger."

"Oh, is he a digger! Right, Buddy?"

"Woof!"

"Well," Grandma suggested, hesitantly because she wasn't handy with tools and fixing things like Pap and Buddy were. "I was thinking. What if she, or he, has a back door?"

Huh?

Pap and Buddy looked to each other.

Back door? Hm.

*   *   *

Cats can be obdurate, stubborn, yes, even mule-headed. And curious, as we have all heard. Yet where does curiosity – as we have all heard – get cats?

Yes; there. We have all heard.

Yet all of us, all of God's creatures, are what we are. A cow by any other name remains a cow, and that goes for Kitty Cat as well.

Cats are curious, or else they are not cats. Add to that, prowling time, and curiosity becomes a quest, an obsession even.

So there it was, like some apocryphal, gravitational, black hole sucking sound, drawing her, insisting, demanding that she follow her most natural inclinations, her most guttural instincts, her greatest urge – to do what?

I can't stand it anymore! I gotta see what those mo-rons next door are up to!

She sat there on the fence post a long time, staring into the darkness. Into the Grunge.

Cats have excellent night vision.

And they are patient.

Her heart beat furiously. She hated it, the fear; but she reveled in it as well, the adrenaline, the visceral rush. Oh, but the fear. Never had it been like this before.

She was safe here, on this side of the fence. She could just stay here and be perfectly fine. Over there, on the other hand, was danger. Mortal peril! Indeed, Kitty had witnessed it, up close, the fury and rage of the big Doberman.

Something, from somewhere, shouted, "No! Don't go!" but Kitty was a cat. She had no choice. She had no choice but to see what those mo-rons were up to over there. So she took a deep breath, and with a graceful bound, once more gained access to The Grunge.

It was dark and creepy here, but she knew the way.

Patience.

Cats are curious and patient.

And stealthy – hopefully.

Chapter Twelve

It was a lovely morning, fit for just about any activity.

Kitty was up a tree, a stubby cabbage palm out in the middle of a pasture. She had been up this tree all night, crammed into the palmetto-bug-infested torture chamber.

Below her, milling about on the ground, were six dogs.

Apparently, Kitty had been neither patient nor stealthy enough. They had been waiting for her. She had been lucky to escape to this tree.

But what escape? To this horrid, horrid refuge – a place from where there was no one to hear her pleas for help?

ME-yow.

Especially now that she was hoarse from meowing all night long.

ME-yow.

*   *   *

Buddy, meanwhile, was singing the Pappy song.

What a Pap, what a Pap, what a Pap, what a mighty good Pa-aaaap ... Mighty, mighty, mighty good Pap ...

Buddy was on his way from the barn, where the kids and Grandma were giving Star a bath and the rest of the "treatment." Buddy didn't get it. Star said the bath and treatment were great. He'd just stand there while Grandma and all the kids gathered around and sprayed him with water and scrubbed him head to toe.

Buddy hated baths himself, which is why he was heading off to see what Pap and Davy were up to, up at the house. Sometimes a bath for Star or Oke turned into a bath for Buddy-boy, too.

He found his pals out back of the house. They had taken some latticework off and Pappy was crouched, looking in the under-the-house with his flashlight.

You guys find anything?

"Not yet."

Buddy could see Davy under there. He crawled in to join him. Davy had a flashlight, too.

"Look to the right there," Pappy said. "Over by that big brick thing, the bottom of the old kitchen fireplace."

Buddy moved forward, joining Davy just as he exclaimed, "Hey, Pap! I think we found something!"

Darned right we did! Buddy agreed. *Look at that!*

"It looks like Grandma's right, Pap!" Davy said. "That old armadillo's got a back door! That's why we can't catch him!"

"A back door," Pappy grumbled. "Diabolical."

Yeah, Buddy concurred. *Diabolical.*

It certainly was earthshaking news.

A few minutes later, the cry came, "Oh, look! Another one!"

By the time they finished, they had found not one back door, but three – and an old jar of homemade pickles that Pap was trying to convince Grandma it was okay to eat because: "Pickles never go bad! I heard they found some in an Egyptian tomb, and they were still just fine!"

They were all standing around in the yard: Pap, Grandma, and an entire tribe of kids. Grandma was holding the old Mason jar that some unknown Loxley had prepared who knows how long ago.

Pap was fuming, but he was coming up with a new plan as well.

Buddy listened as Pap made several proposals as to what they should do next.

Grandma had a question: "Does it really matter if she, or he, lives under the house?"

Buddy could not believe what he was hearing. Pappy, obviously, couldn't either, not to mention Davy.

"Of course, it matters!" Pap declared with all the conviction of a well-compensated TV preacher.

"I don't know," Grandma wondered. "What could be the worst that could happen?"

"Yeah, Pappy," Annie said. "What could be the worst that could happen?"

Pap was flabbergasted.

"Why ... why, the whole, entire house could sink! Into oblivion!!"

Oblivion did not sound good to Buddy. Grandma, however, was clearly unconvinced.

Ask about the leprosy? Buddy prodded. *Remind her of the leprosy. And cooties! Cooties, too!*

"And," Pap said, as if he had thought of it himself, "what about leprosy?"

Grandma rolled her eyes. Obviously, she was not convinced of that either, or very concerned over it.

"Hey, kids!" she said. "Who wants to go in and make some cookies?!"

Buddy could not believe it. It was like no one cared about the rampaging armadillo, or Pap's predicament. No, they only cheered and followed Grandma around the house as if she were the Pied Piper of Scrumptious Treats Galore.

It was clear Davy wanted to make cookies, too.

"Go on," Pap said, and Davy dashed off to catch up to the cookie makers.

Pap, a look of consternation on his face, stared under the house.

Buddy did as well.

So, Buddy opined, *I guess they'll all be making cookies ... in the kitchen.*

Pap, his consternation glowering from his wise, but weary, eyes, looked at Buddy.

With a sigh of utter doom and ultimate failure, he mumbled, "Go ahead, Buddy. I reckon they're gonna need some help in there."

Buddy wanted to stay with Pap to comfort him. He really did.

But ... *No time for that! They probably already started the oven!!*

So off Buddy went. There was nothing more fun than helping make cookies with Grandma and the kids. He paused, however, as he went around the corner of the old wash house. He looked back.

Poor old Pap.

Darned armadilly.

*   *   *

The Sinister Six were in a quandary.

They had Kitty. There was no way she was getting away.

Still, they had no way of getting up the tree to her.

They were, at the moment, attempting to make a ladder. It didn't have to be a big one. It was a relatively young cabbage palm, maybe fifteen feet.

It had taken some work, but they finally got the necessary lumber, hammer, and nails over to tree.

"Bloimy!" Cornwall declared. "Oi can't 'old onto this 'ammer! Oi ain't got no bloody 'ands!"

It seemed to be the consensus. To get the job done, they needed hands.

"Oh, lookee, lookee!" Vic said, excitedly. "I can use zhe side of my head to drive zhe nail!"

The other dogs watched, and winced.

WHACK!! WHACK!! WHACK!!

"Darn it! I keep bending zhe nail!"

"All right, all right," Lionel said. "This isn't working. He set his hands on his hips and looked up into the tree at the black and white cat crammed between a mass of palm fonds.

"I just know I can climb it," Ali, the boxer, insisted. "Just look at all those big spiky things coming out. It's like a natural ladder."

"You've already tried that," Lionel said. "Like, a thousand times."

"*Sí*. You tried eet already."

"But I was doing it wrong before," Ali said. "Watch this."

She leaped to her feet. She studied the tree.

"See? I was putting my feet right on the spiky things, see? But what I really need to do is keep them inside, away from the front edge and kind of hug the tree as I move up, one spiky thing at a time. See?"

And there she went. Everyone watched. Lots of rolling of eyes.

Actually, she was doing pretty good this time. Maybe Ali was right. They had been doing it wrong.

They all moved onto their haunches. They were hopeful; ears perked.

She was really doing it, slowly, one step at a time.

Then at about five feet it happened, real fast-like. It was hard to say exactly what it was, the fatal error, but all of a sudden Ali was upside down, her foot caught in a broken cabbage palm boot hole.

"Owww, ouch, ouch, ouch, ouch, ouch!"

She was yelping and carrying on.

"Owww, ouch, ouch, ouch, ouch, ouch!"

After a minute or two of everyone shaking their heads, they managed to get her down.

Ali didn't seem badly injured, just out of breath. A minute later, she was all better.

"I think I know what I was doing wrong this time," she said.

Lionel rolled his eyes. He glanced up at the cat, looking down at them.

"You think that's funny, don't you, Cat?"

"Can't say it's not," was the reply.

"Smart-alecky cat," Lionel mumbled. Then he said, "Come on, fellas. We gotta think of something. Put your thinking caps on." He glanced at Vic. He scratched his head. "It's uh … just a saying, Vic. We don't really have thinking caps."

"'Ey, Oi gots a oidea!" Cornwall said. "Oi saw it on a circus show once. It's called the 'uman bloody pyramid."

"*Sí*. I have seen that before," Ernesto concurred.

"But," Vic interjected, "ve are not humans."

"No," Lionel said. "Don't you get it, Vic? We'll build a *canine* pyramid."

"A canine pyramid," the others repeated. "Good idea."

"*Yavol*! Gudt idea!"

*   *   *

I love cookies.

Buddy loved cookies.

Little Paul had dropped his and was not fast enough to get them before someone – you know who – snatched them up and gobbled them down.

Pappy was back on schedule, which meant Buddy was as well.

Buddy thought it had been an exceptionally nice day, a splendid day, in fact. He couldn't put his finger on it, but everything had seemed so, so bright and right today. He was down in his "private" hole under the porch. The hard, butt-packed sand gave him a level of comfort and security.

Buddy had never imagined there were so many tunnels under the house. He never went under there by himself. It was too spooky and creepy, with all those cobwebs, and spiders lurking in the corners.

He was taking a moment to reflect on the day.

I love cookies.

He rolled over and got comfortable. The cool under-the-porch sand felt good. It was good to have a place for contemplation and restful slumber – a place for him, no one else, just for Buddy.

He heard a familiar scratching – digging – sound.

He cringed. He told himself to ignore it.

Don't roll over. Just don't look. Maybe he, or she, will go away.

But he had to. He looked over his shoulder, and there it was: that goofy smile.

"Hi! I'm Harlan!"

Buddy resisted the urge to run away. He did, however, scoot back a little.

"Yeah. I know that."

"Well, last time I was here, I didn't know if you heard me, you ran away so fast."

"Right, well, I don't know if I actually *ran away*."

The ball of cooties shrugged.

"So," Buddy said, "do you want something? I mean, this is the second time you put a hole in my wall."

"Oh," Harlan looked around. "Sorry. You want me to fix it?"

"No, no, no," Buddy replied. "Just tell me what you want."

"Well, I was actually gonna tell you this morning, but I fell asleep. I was all grubbed out when I got home, if you know what I'm sayin'. Anyway, I just thought you'd want to know that they've got your friend!"

"My friend?"

"Yeah. The cat."

"Uh, she's not really my friend. But what do you mean? Who's got her?"

"Those whacked out maniacs next door, that's who. They've had her treed ever since last night."

Buddy didn't really consciously think it, but the thought occurred: *So that's why everything felt so right all day today.*

He also felt a flood of concern well up in his belly, however, and he wondered: *Concern over Kitty? How can that be?*

But it was.

"So, she's still up that tree?"

"Last I looked," Harlan said. Then, "Give me a few," and he scurried off.

A few minutes later, he returned, winded.

"She's," he said, breathing hard, "she's not good. She's still up there. Hasn't had any water. I don't guess she can last much longer."

Buddy scowled.

Harlan went on. "It's that lone cabbage out in the Grunge pasture. From the looks of it, those whackadoodles over there have something planned."

"Oh? What?"

"Heck if I know, but it reminds me of a circus act I once saw."

Buddy didn't know what to think. He didn't know if he could trust this ... Harlan character.

"All right," he said. "I'll check it out, um ... ... *Mister* Armadillo?"

"That's what they call me," Harlan replied.

Buddy crawled out of his under-the-porch and took in the situation. All normal. He did not want to sound the alarm or make a scene, if this turned out to be some kind of scam. After all, Harlan might be sending him on some wild goose chase so he could take over his under-the-porch and convert it into a cootie factory.

It was true, though. He had not seen Kitty since yesterday. Buddy even heard Grandma say she didn't come in for breakfast this morning. That wasn't so unusual, though. Kitty could be gone a good while sometimes. Who knew where?

"Where ya goin', Buddy?" Pap said from his hot bathtub as he trotted past.

Oh ... nowhere. I'll be back before you know it.

A few minutes later, Buddy was at the fence-line, peering through the woods, towards the Grunge pasture.

"Can't see anything from here," he grumbled.

He headed down the fence-line, listening. He was almost to Icky Springs, passing by some saw palmetto, his nose to the ground and ears attuned, when –

"HEY THERE!!"

Buddy nearly leaped out of his skin.

"Come on, man! Do you have to sneak up on me like that?!"

"Oh. Sorry," Harlan said.

Buddy rolled his eyes. "So, are you sure they've got Kitty treed over there?"

"Oh, yes. In that lone palm on the other side of the rise."

Buddy sighed. "The other side of the rise," he mumbled. He tugged at the fence with his paw. "I've gotta get over there."

"Maybe I can help," Harlan said.

"You?" Buddy muttered with an amused chuckle. "I don't think you're gonna fit me into one of your tunnels."

"I don't suppose so," Harlan agreed. He looked around suspiciously and lowered his voice. "All right, here's the deal."

Buddy wondered, *Who does this guy think he is?*

Harlan looked around again, and said, "If anyone asks, you did not see this. Not that they would believe you anyway."

So Buddy watched, first with curiosity, then with skepticism, then with fascination followed by wonder. Finally, his jaw dropped in disbelief as the heavily armored, creepy, prehistoric creature grabbed the wire fence with his two hands and ripped it apart like it was made of the proverbial paper maché.

Except for "Uhhhh," Buddy was speechless.

"You should be able to make it through there," Harlan said, "and remember, this is our little secret. It's best for our species that no one knows of our super strength."

"Uhhhh ... yeah. I ... I suppose so," Buddy mumbled. "So ... that's how you got out of that trap that time? Super ... strength?"

Harlan shrugged modestly.

Buddy looked on with outright stupefaction.

"So, then," Harlan said, "I guess I'll see you out there in the pasture. I have an access on the rise out there in a patch of palmetto. You can't miss it." Then he was gone, back down the hole.

Buddy stared a moment. Then off he bounded, through the hole in the fence and onto the neighbor's property.

It was the first time he had ever set foot on The Grunge. It felt wrong somehow. Pappy had said to never go over there. But he was worried ... worried about Kitty?

He wondered, *How can this be?*

But it was.

Chapter Thirteen

"I cannot believe this. I am literally surrounded by mo-rons."

It was true. Kitty was surrounded by six of them.

That was not counting the one in the tree – her.

Kitty was berating herself: "I just had ta see what d'ey was doin' over here, didn't I? Well, I guess I found out."

It was getting bad. She was terribly hungry, not to mention, thirsty. This was not the kind of thirsty you get after consuming the most scrumpty parts of a rat, but the kind you get right before you have kidney failure and die.

"If I'm gonna make a break for it, I'd better do it soon, while I still have the strength."

Kitty was talking to herself in a low, rumbly, pre-delirium grumble.

Her only hope was that they really were the mo-rons they appeared to be. There had been no opportunity for escape. Well, there had been while they were occupied with bringing the lumber, nails, and hammer over, but she had wimped out.

Kitty was wedged into the slick, edgy, hard-to-manage, easy-to-get-stuck-in fronds of this awful, hideous tree. She could see the fence-line from here. She could even see their barn and parts of the house.

It seemed so far away.

She told herself to just do it, to just leap from the tree and run for it, just as she had been telling herself without pause ever since the moment they chased her up it last night.

It seemed so long ago.

"Just do it! Run!" she told herself. But she couldn't.

Vic really scared her. That one meant business.

Why do I have ta be so stinkin' curious?!

She sighed. "Because I'm a cat, d'at's why. But d'en," she looked down at the maniacs below, "it's still better d'an d'at."

The ladder attempt had been more amusing than unsettling, all of them standing around looking at their paws with ludicrous expressions on their faces. This was different, though. It was still amusing, in a way, because they were such … mo-rons.

She could not believe what she was seeing. Worse, it might actually work.

Yes, it appeared that the canine pyramid might actually work.

It was impressive. Kitty had not imagined Vic could be so strong that he could support the weight of the other five dogs – including Cornwall. She couldn't quite see

Vic, buried under the pile of dogs as he was, but she could hear him grunting in German.

Yes, he was doing it. They were all doing it.

Kitty, meanwhile, was growing nervous.

There had been a learning curve. Their first attempts had been nothing less than hilarious. But they had kept on practicing and figuring out better methods. They were within feet of her now. She had already retreated to the highest frond wedge she could squeeze herself into – and hopefully out of.

Kitty was growing truly fearful.

They had by now erected a half of a canine pyramid, more like a canine ramp, or right triangle, going up the side of the tree; biggest to smallest: Vic on the bottom, Ernesto on top with Viper standing on his head, barking and snapping at Kitty, and coming much, much too close.

"Hey!" Kitty heard someone, the beagle, suggest. "What if we dig a hole?!"

"A hole?" the others replied. "How's that gonna help?"

That's what Kitty wondered.

"We don't use the hole," Lionel said. "We pile the dirt at the base of the tree and use that. It will give us the extra couple feet we need."

The dogs all barked their enthusiasm. Then they broke down the half pyramid in an experienced and orderly manner and immediately went to digging, building a ramp.

Kitty could not believe it. She knew exactly what would happen. They would brag about it to everyone, and they would all know how she came to her end.

She could hear them now: "It was curiosity that killed that cat!"

Oh, the ignominy!

She had to do something. Maybe now was the time, while they were all busy digging. Except Ernesto, who was a bad digger, had been put in charge of watching her.

"Look away, ya stupid three-legged dog," she mumbled under her breath. "Look somewhere else!"

She glared at him, at his beady little eyes fixed on her.

The new ramp got bigger and bigger. They finished excavating, then started packing it down. A moment later, they all took their positions, one at a time, constructing the canine half-pyramid.

It seemed much, much too close.

Here came Viper, dashing to the top of the pile. The annoying yapper leaped and snapped so that Kitty had to take a swipe at her.

Whoa! D'at was much too close.

Yes, it looked like this was the end for Kitty.

Just do it! Scramble! Leap and run! Run! Now! NOW!! RUN FOR YOUR LIFE!!!

She took some deep breaths and a few obstructed, less than optimum, stretches. There was no longer another option.

Kitty said a short cat prayer: *Please, God. Crush them ta dust.*

She took another deep breath and told herself: *All right. Here goes.*

At that moment, something caught her eye, at the top of the rise, at the palmetto patch there. Yes, it was him, the vile but helpful cootie carrier … and … and who was that with him?

Kitty's heart swelled. It soared. Never had she seen such a glorious sight. There he was, her knight in brown, furry armor – Buddy-boy! He had come to her rescue.

Not that Kitty needed rescuing; she was just about to make her escape anyway.

Yet it was only Buddy, one against six.

That didn't really matter, though. His presence alone would give her time to get away. Yes, she would be free of these insane nutballs, and she would never come back here again as long as she lived!

Then Kitty felt something strange and foreign, squiggling up from deep inside. She couldn't just leave Buddy there to fight the Sinister Six. Could she?

Eh. A cat's gotta do what a cat's gotta do.

She watched intently, while at the same time hissing and swiping at Viper, who was a lot tougher and more athletic than she had expected.

Buddy and Harlan appeared to be making plans.

What plans?! Just charge! Come on! Just charge! CHARGE!! Rip d'ose nutballs limb from limb! COME ON!!

But the rescue squad just stood there while Viper, meanwhile, was getting dangerously close. Not to mention the incessant yapping! *Oh, my gosh! And right in my ear!*

Finally, it looked like they were taking action. Kitty watched with fascination, disbelief even, as Harlan rolled into a ball and Buddy picked him up, as if he were bowling. Then, with a good running start, he gave Harlan the old heave ho.

Fascination would be an understatement.

The cootie-infused bowling ball seemed unstoppable, looming ever larger and more menacing as it hurled down the rise, gathering speed and some serious kinetic energy, barreling right for the canine half-pyramid.

"Hey!" someone shouted from below. "What's that coming right towards us?!"

"Oh, no!" someone else cried, but by that time it was too late. The pyramid wobbled. It quaked with jittery anticipation, but only momentarily because the barreling, cootie-infused bowling ball made calamitous contact, sending assorted canines flying in just as many directions before it continued past, down the hill, directly into a cootie hole.

STEE-RIKE!!

"YIPPEE!!" Kitty shouted, and, wasting no time, she was down the tree and gone, passing Buddy on the way. When she reached the top of the rise, she looked back to observe the free-for-all.

Buddy was in trouble. Six against one.

It looked like one of those old time Kung Fu movies.

Kitty got that strange feeling again, like maybe she should do something – like maybe help. Buddy, after all, had just come to her rescue.

She was debating this in her mind when she heard a big *WHAP-CRUNCH!* from the direction of the farm. Then she heard another and another. Kitty dashed over the rise to see Okee Donkey charging up the hill.

"YIPPEE!" Kitty shouted. "HURRAY!" she cried as Oke dashed past. "Go get 'em, big boy!!"

Kitty thought he gave her a look as he passed, but that didn't matter because off he charged, down the hill, scattering dogs to the winds.

It was a beautiful thing.

"Go! GO!" Kitty shouted, encouraging them onward. "Make mincemeat out of 'em!"

But it was to no avail.

"Great," she grumbled. "Just like Lee at Gettysburg."

A few minutes later, Buddy and Oke trudged up the hill, a little out of breath but no missing limbs or digits or anything like that.

"Nice goin', fellas," Kitty said.

Dog and Donkey looked at one another and kept on walking.

"Hey … Guys," Kitty said, following along. "Come on. I was just keepin' a eye on 'em. For you guys. And did ya know d'ey was plannin' on kidnappin' Davy?"

Dog and donkey turned.

Buddy frowned. "And when were you gonna tell us that?"

"Oh … uh … soon. Real soon," Kitty mumbled.

She followed along, back home, flicking her tail, like cats do.

*   *   *

"Where ya goin', Buddy?" Pap said as he trotted past.

Oh … nowhere. Buddy replied. *I'll be back before you know it.*

Pappy was working on his novel.

No one had perfected relaxation like Pap had. A beer and a hot tub was all it really took.

And a loyal, royal hound at his side, of course.

"I wonder where Buddy took off to in such a hurry," Pap mumbled under his breath.

His mind went back to the time of his ancestors and all those stories he grew up hearing. Nothing soothed old Pap's aching bones and weary mind like a pleasant stroll backwards through time.

He paused to scratch something underwater. Back to work.

His moment of calm and respite was, unfortunately, abruptly shattered by a big *WHAP-CRUNCH!*

Pap's contented, bald brow crinkled disconsolately. He pushed his straw hat back. His entire body cringed. It convulsed.

"Oh, no. Not again."

But there it came. Another big *WHAP-CRUNCH!* followed a moment later by another.

"That does it," Pap grouched, and he got up from his comfortable relaxation, wrapped his towel around himself, slapped on his shower shoes, and stomped off towards the pasture.

"Danged donkey," he grumbled as he gingerly climbed over the wood-slat fence."

*   *   *

Buddy was holding down the broken wire fence so Oke could get over it.

"That's tricky stuff," Oke mentioned. "I almost took a tumble on the way out, you know."

"You can't be too careful," Buddy said.

"That's for sure," Oke replied.

Oke was almost there when they noticed they were not alone.

"What the heck goes on out here?!" Pap declared, dripping wet towel, hands on scrawny hips.

Oke and Buddy looked around.

There was no sign of Kitty.

What could they do but shrug?

Chapter Fourteen

The next day

They were on their late afternoon walk – not to be confused with the early afternoon walk or the mid-afternoon version.

This was the big one. The one with a sunset attached.

Grandma and Buddy and the kids – and anyone else who wanted to tag along, even Pap sometimes – would head out to the hill on the other side of the lake to watch the evening colors.

Big skies make for big sunsets.

From here, the barn and house were to the right; the cypress slough, Icky Springs, and the fence-line were to the left, and before them was wide, open pasture.

It was a perfect sunset. Yet, what is perfect?

"Is that the prettiest sunset you've ever seen, Grandma?" little Timmy asked.

"Why, I don't think I can say, sweetie," Grandma said.

They were gathered on the park bench and picnic table and beach blanket.

Buddy didn't really get it, sunsets, but Grandma always brought snacks along, so sunset time was okay with him. It was possible that it even outranked Pap and hot bathtub time. As an added bonus, there was little chance that Grandma might grab a hose and declare, "BATH TIME!" or whip out her nail clippers or some other unseemly torture.

"They're all beautiful," Grandma went on. "The beauty is in their differences, children. Every sunset, and sunrise, is different. Every one is beautiful, in its own way – just like all of you."

"So," little Connie asked, "how come we don't come out for sunrise time?"

"Because those are mornings," Grandma replied. "There's much too much to do in the mornings."

"That's right," Davy said. "You've seen how much Grandma does, from the time she gets up way before us in the morning, when it's still dark outside?"

Annie tilted her head. "Pappy says Grandma is the reason he gets up in the morning. First, because he loves her and adores her, and without her he would have no reason to get up, and he would have to find a cliff and throw himself off of it."

"What's second?" little Jack asked.

"Oh," Annie said, "because Grandma makes him get out of bed so she can make it."

Everyone giggled. Sunset time was fun.

Grandma had brought buckeyes for snack, so Buddy was enjoying himself, too, licking kid's fingers and faces.

*   *   *

Ahhhh.

Pap was soaking in the hot bathtub, experiencing relief for aching bones and a weary mind. The fence was repaired. All was good on the farm. Life was good.

Ahhhh.

"Watch your step there, Big Boy. This tub ain't big enough for the both of us, ya know. Ha, ha, ha, ha, ha!"

Across the way

"Whoy, look at what Oi found over 'ere!" Cornwall shouted. He was standing at the fence-line, near Icky Springs. "Ya won't believe it, mates!"

From under the big oak tree next to the pasture, someone shouted, "What is it?!"

"Just come on over and take a look-see. Ya won't believe it!"

A few minutes later, the others showed up.

"All right, all right," Lionel said. "What's such a big deal that we all gotta see it?"

With a proud grin, Cornwall pointed.

"Look at what Oi found."

Five sets of eyes grew wide.

"Holy smokes!"

"*Ay caramba!*"

"Oh, lookee! How did zhat big hole get zhere?"

"Does it matter?" Lionel said. "It's a hole in the fence."

"A hole in the fence." Everyone repeated it, as if it were some mystical pronouncement.

They stared a minute.

Then Vic said, "Chickens."

"Yeah. Chickens."

Six sets of salivary glands kicked into overdrive.

Chickens!

They all looked at each other, then the hole.

Vic gave the command: "To the chickens!"

With that, he bolted for the hole, the others following right behind, shouting, "To the chickens! Death to chickens! Chickens taste delicious!"

*   *   *

Ahhhh.
Pap was soaking in all the goodness of a fine, well-constructed life.
Double Ahhhh.
Pap took his hat and glasses off and submerged himself, feet sticking out one end, his nose out the other. The sounds of the world were dampened, remote, some of them obliterated.
Hm. That's a strange sound.
Pap dismissed it. Then –
Hm. What is that sound?
Curiosity got the best of him, and he surfaced.
"Those dogs sound mighty close," he mumbled as he dried off his head and put his hat on, then his glasses. His eyes grew wide.
"SON OF A … DAG-NABBIT!!" he cried at the sight of mad dogs scattering Grandma's chickens. Feathers, they were flying!
In an instant, he was up and out of the tub, wrapping the towel around himself.
"GIT!" he cried. "Bad dogs!" Then, "BUDDY!!"
He started for the melee over at the barnyard, stopped to put his shower shoes on, then off he dashed.
He came back for his bristly scrub-brush-poker-thing.
Then off he dashed again, shouting, "BUDDY!! BUDDY-BOY!!"
As he ran around the turnout fence, he could see Oke growing anxious, snorting and stomping and looking awfully cantankerous.
"Stay in there, Oke!" Pap shouted. "You dogs get out of here! BUDDY-BOY!" and, No, Oke! Don't you bust that fence!"

*   *   *

Buddy was out on the hill, stretched out on a beach blanket with the kids, licking fingers and faces and enjoying the unearthly rapture of the full-belly extravaganza: *Double Ahhhhhh.*
The sun was just going down in a truly spectacular display. All sunsets are beautiful, yes, but not all are spectacular.
Buddy was soaking in the goodness of a fine, well-constructed life. He was starting to doze along the way.

90

Grandma was talking about the shapes of the clouds when Annie said, "Are those dogs supposed to be over here?"

Dogs? Over here? What dogs?

Buddy sat up just as Grandma cried. "Oh, no! What are those dogs doing over here?!"

Darn it! Buddy had forgotten all about the hole in the fence.

Instantly, he was on his feet.

"No, Buddy!" Grandma shouted, but Buddy was already gone. He had a job to do. A minute later, he was passing Icky Springs at a gallop. He glanced at the hole in the fence. That was about the time he heard it.

"BUDDY!!"

Pappy needed him.

"BUDDY-BOY!!"

He dashed around the lake and down the pasture fence towards the barn. Around he came. Kitty was there, loitering and appearing to smoke a cigarette. She nodded down the other fence-line.

"D'ey went d'at a'way."

Buddy had just missed them!

But there they were! Out in the pasture! Pappy was chasing the dogs chasing the chickens, and Oke was stuck in the turnout, snorting and stomping.

Buddy's first impulse was to charge through the turnout, but he wasn't allowed in there, so he ran around the other way.

"WOOF!!" he barked.

Into the pasture he charged, just in time to see Oke bust down the fence between the turnout and the pasture.

"WOOF!!"

"HEE-HAWWW!!

Pappy was still chasing dogs with his scrub-brush-poker-thing while yelling at Oke, "Bad donkey!"

With the arrival of Oke, however, the dogs gave up the chase and cleared out of the pasture.

Buddy and Pap followed, Buddy overtaking Pap, who was slowing down and having trouble running in his shower shoes and unbecomingly climbing over the fence. The towel got stuck. He had to go back for it.

All the while, he was shouting behind him, "You best not tear that fence down, Oke! I mean it!"

*   *   *

Grandma was beside herself.

"You kids wait here!" she instructed, and off she sprinted.

She wasn't as good a runner as she was forty years ago, but she did all right.

The closer she came, the worse it sounded. Then, suddenly, it got worse: yes, not only were Pap screaming and the dogs barking, there were those sickening sounds of dogs fighting.

She looked behind her.

"I said stay there!"

The kids all froze.

Grandma desperately looked around for a weapon as she ran. There! There was something! A stick laying on the ground! By the pump station!

She grabbed it. It yanked her backwards.

OOF!!

"Really?!"

Really. It wasn't a stick. It was an old, almost broken root.

She yanked at it, mumbling some things she might not want kids, who happened to be standing right there, to hear.

"What are you kids doing here?! I told you to stay back there!"

They all watched while Grandma yanked, grunted, sweated, and finally wrestled it loose. Then off she went, though at a more subdued, gaspy clip.

"You kids stay right there!" she yelled over her shoulder.

She could see it now, the battle. It raged, and she knew not what to do.

But do something she would.

CHARGE!!

*   *   *

Marv observed the field of battle from several vantage points.

It was the biggest action he'd seen in a while, probably since the coyote incident.

As the only eye witness, Marv was aware of the truth in that matter. He had remained mum, however, out of respect for Okee Donkey. He was a good boy, after all.

Regardless, he followed the battle as it transpired, chronicling it in his head for a potential, upcoming ballad.

At first, it was pandemonium as Pap was chasing dogs chasing chickens, but then Buddy showed up, and Oke busted down the turnout fence, and the dogs dispersed.

It had been clear from where Marv sat, however, that the battle was not yet won.

The forces of Evil regrouped at the fence-line, just west of Icky Springs. They stood their ground as the forces of Good made their advance, Buddy leading the charge, leaving the commander, Pap, far to his rear.

Marv would have recommended waiting for reinforcements, but there was no stopping Buddy. He charged right into the middle of them: six against one.

"DON'T YOU BUST THAT FENCE DOWN, OKE!" Pappy shouted from the rear.

A dogfight is about as vicious a display of carnal violence as nature provides.

Buddy swooped in with a flying chop kick, taking all of them by surprise. He focused on Vic, the big one, knocking him to the ground and addling him good.

The horde regrouped. They swarmed.

The little one had Buddy by the tail, but Buddy couldn't be bothered because the boxer, Ali, was throwing short, stinging punches. It was clear Buddy had little chance in a boxing match with a boxer, but then he managed to grab Ali's fist. He spun and flipped her over his shoulder, then clunked her in the face, knocking her cuckoo. Meanwhile, the little one still had him by the tail, and the three-legged one had him by a back leg.

Buddy kept shaking it, but he wouldn't let go.

The fat one, who seemed mostly interested in egging the others on, stepped up, and took a swing at Buddy; but the big, brown dog deflected it and gave him a karate chop to the head.

KONK!

Cornwall staggered.

Then he started crying, and backing up, and saying, "Oh, yeah?! Troiy ta get me now! Troiy ta get me now!" and he kept backing up and jumping out of the way. It was obviously a delaying tactic, giving Vic time to launch another barrage.

Oh, and it was brutal. The two little dogs were still hanging onto Buddy's tail and leg, while the beagle had by now grabbed onto the other back leg, so Buddy was fighting Vic while at the same time trying to shake all three of them loose.

The other two, Cornwall and Ali, were barking and snapping and trying to get to his forelegs.

Buddy, however, was busy using those – and expertly by the way.

Bap, bap, bap!

Py-YAAA!!

Vic was tough, though. He shook it off and delivered a solid, discombobulating haymaker, knocking Buddy for a loop and sending him and the three attached dogs rolling down the hill, nearly into Icky Springs. But Buddy was up again – dogs still attached. He leaped at Vic with a roundhouse kick, sending him soaring into the fence.

By now, Pap was on the scene. So was Grandma, from the other direction.

"GIT! BAD DOGS!" Pap was shouting at them, and over his shoulder, "DON'T YOU BUST THAT FENCE DOWN, OKE!"

Grandma, meanwhile, screamed: "GIT! BAD DOGS!" and over her shoulder, "I TOLD YOU KIDS TO STAY BACK!"

93

The battle raged, moving right into Icky Springs – which was called that for a darned good reason.

Marv was impressed.

Pap did not hesitate. He charged right in there, into the deep, messy muck, his scrub-brush-poker-thing held high in valor. The first thing that happened, though, was that his foot got stuck in the mud, real deep, and when he pulled his foot out, he realized the shower shoe was gone.

He locked eyes with Grandma, who was standing by, screaming at dogs and kids.

"I'll get it later!" Pap shouted.

With that, he dove into the dog pile, which consisted of one dog for each of Buddy's appendages, tail included, plus Vic leading the full, frontal assault.

Yes, Buddy was literally surrounded, six against one.

Still, he was standing his ground: a fighting machine. He blocked a lame roundhouse and came from under with a devastating punch to Vic's narrow, peanut-brain-sized, hard-as-a-hammer head. *DING!!*

And another. *DING!!*

Oh, what a fighting machine!

Meanwhile, just down the way, Oke was in a tizzy, snorting and stomping around in frenzied, rampageful circles.

"DON'T YOU BUST THAT FENCE DOWN, OKE!!"

Finally, Pap was there, fully engaged in the heat of battle, which had moved to the unsung, sloppy shores of Icky Springs.

The first thing he did was grab the tiny one and toss her over the fence. Then he did the same to the three-legged one. With the beagle, he tried the same maneuver, but he couldn't get the dog's mouth unclenched from Buddy's leg, so Pap bit him.

YELP!!

That did it. The beagle released his grip, and Pap grabbed him by the scruff and tail and tossed him over the fence.

That helped for a minute, but the dogs simply dashed back through the hole and were quickly back in the fray.

"DAG-NABBIT!!"

Grandma analyzed the situation. She moved her forces forward.

"YOU KIDS STAY BACK!"

Without being ordered to, she made a command decision and took over the tossing of dogs over the fence so Pappy could deploy his assets elsewhere.

Marv had never been so impressed, so enthralled, as he was with Grandma, especially after she moved her forces in a skillfully deployed, oblique flanking maneuver, consolidating and cutting the three little dogs off at the hole in the fence, all the while continuing to shout over her shoulder, "YOU KIDS STAY BACK!"

Buddy and Pap, meanwhile, continued the fight.

Pap had the fat one cornered, utilizing his scrub-brush-poker-thing to fend him off. Then, masterfully, like a bolt of lightning, his other hand shot out and snatched the overweight dog by the scruff. He lugged him out of the black morass, up the bank, and over to the hole. Fattie was yelping and cussing in Cockney the entire way as Pap hauled him over to the hole and unceremoniously shoved him through.

"HOO!!"

Pap wiped his brow, replacing sweat with icky muck.

He and Grandma looked at each other, knowingly, with congratulations.

But, no time for that! And Pap left her there to guard the opening with her broken-off root.

The four dogs snarled, barked, and threatened, but Gandma stood firm, shaking her root at them menacingly, while shouting over her shoulder, "YOU KIDS STAY BACK!"

Pap was back in the black slop in a second. With this one, the boxer, he would have to be wary. They sparred a while, then Pap made a feinting move. And Ali fell for it!

Marv couldn't get enough. By now, in fact, everyone else had shown up: Emory the hawk and pretty much every bird within earshot. Squirrels, rabbits, anoles, frogs, grasshoppers, and ants appeared. Even the lowly armadillo cheered on the heroes from the sidelines.

The boxer didn't stand a chance against a fully enraged and well-armed Pap. He seemed a master swordsman out there: parry, feint, thrust, feint, parry, parry, feint, and THRUST!

"DON'T YOU BUST THAT FENCE DOWN, OKE!!"

"This will make an award-winning ballad!" Marv mumbled to himself.

"What did you say, Pop?!"

"Oh, hello, son."

"Pretty good fight, huh?"

"It is that, son. Now pay attention. You might learn something about … about standing on your own two feet."

"Uh, not sure what that has to do with this, Pop. But … whatever you say."

It wasn't but another minute that Pap, looking like an old-time lion tamer, had the boxer backed through the hole.

He turned his attention to Vic and Buddy.

CHARGE!!

Into the mucky donnybrook he strode, conviction and righteousness on his side, his scrub-brush-poker-thing held high.

Buddy and Vic, meanwhile, were rolling around in the mud. It looked like Buddy had Vic in a headlock, but it was difficult to tell who was who. Pap was after the one without a tail, which was the appendage he most naturally went for – except there wasn't a whole lot of grabbing room there.

"DANG IT!" Then he shouted over his shoulder, "DON'T YOU BUST THAT FENCE DOWN, OKE!!"

And from over at the hole in the fence, "YOU KIDS STAY BACK!"

Having no noteworthy tail to grab hold of, Pap went for Vic's back legs, and he had them!

"So! How'd'ya like that?!" Pap, now as mucky as the embittered foes, shouted. "It ain't so much fun, is it, mister?!"

Then something happened. Pappy lost his grip and slipped into the mud – his feet reaching for the sky. The dogs took the fight up the bank.

Pap struggled to get out – and to locate his missing towel.

Meanwhile, all looked on in wonder and awe as it became clear that Buddy did not need anyone's help, not when it was one against one.

Bang! Ding! Ow!

Vic didn't have a chance. The big dumb Doberman was yelping and crying and trying to escape the furious fists of Buddy-boy.

Buddy took a minute just to slap him around a little and call him uncomplimentary names.

Then Pappy was back, as inky black as Icky Springs itself, charging forward, wielding his scrub-brush-poker-thing in one hand and clutching his black, mucky, soppy towel with the other.

By now, everyone knew it was over.

Vic was pathetic.

He was crying, "Don't hurt me! Don't hurt me! I'm leafing! I'm leafing!"

Buddy and Pap didn't let up, though. They chased him around the yard a couple times more until Vic finally dashed for the hole in the fence, Grandma showing him the way with her broken-off root, and making sure to give him a good whack on the butt with it as he passed through.

Buddy wasn't done, though. He followed behind, staying right on Vic's tucked stump and the others' tucked tails until they all disappeared into the woods.

A few minutes later, Buddy re-emerged. He looked tired and beat up pretty good; but just then came a rousing cheer from all quarters, from the treetops and the telephone wires to the woods and beyond – even from a cootie hole under a nearby palmetto.

Taking stock in the situation, Buddy turned once more and released one last "WOOF!" of warning.

To all those gathered, victory shone about them like a shining city on the hill. Yes, the Sinister Six were gone, Gone with the Woof.

Everyone, Grandma and the kids, cheered and celebrated.

Buddy, meanwhile, like any self-respecting hero, waved modestly.

Everyone was happy but Pap, who grumbled, "You all stay here while I go get some stuff ta fix this danged fence. Come on, Buddy," he said, and the two muddy, buddy warriors headed back to the barn.

On the way, Oke came out to greet them.

Nice job fellas.

"Good boy, Oke," Pappy mumbled.

Yeah, Buddy agreed. *Good boy, Oke.*

*   *   *

From some distance, perched on a fencepost, Kitty watched with interest.

"Not bad. Not bad at all." She glanced up at the telephone line at two mockingbirds, father and son. "Now, if we could only put a stopper on d'at pesky kid."

Chapter Fifteen

Elwood got up at his usual time, right after Pap and Buddy came in from their last foray into the outside night. He yawned and stretched. It was nice here, in the box that said "Vacuum Cleaner Bags." He had personalized it, fixed it up a little, with some napkins and other soft, fluffy items. There was plenty to choose from around here.

Life had never been so good for Elwood.

He had awakened during the day to several fanciful aromas, one of which was chocolate chip cookies. That would be his first stop tonight, the cookie jar. Oh, and Pap had finally brought bananas home from the store. Elwood had heard Grandma reminding him after he forgot them last time.

Good old Grandma.

Elwood stopped at the bathroom.

"Oh! That's a nice surprise. New cat box litter. Hm. Mountain Wildflower Scent." He finished brushing his teeth, then headed off to "work"; he had a big night planned of foraging and living large.

*   *   *

Squirrels are diurnal creatures, normally, but that does not mean they sleep just because it is nighttime.

The night owls, led by Artie Darwin, were still awake. They were all keyed up in fact, still agog over the great battle of the day. No one liked the Sinister Six. They were just like raccoons, except they barked and didn't have hands.

Everyone had heard about it, all up and down the County Road, all the way over to the river and beyond even. Many of the clan had come out to witness it from the roof of the barn. It was already being called the Battle of Icky Springs.

Chloe laughed. "And did you see the look on Pap's face when Grandma took over tossing the short dogs over the fence?!"

Haaa, ha, ha, ha, ha!! Everyone laughed.

"Whoa!" Halsey shouted with glee. "Pap was one proud dude, dude!"

"Or," Kimmie giggled, "how about when Pappy and Buddy were chasing Vic in circles, and Vic was crying, 'Don't hurt me! Don't hurt me!'"

Haaa, ha, ha, ha, ha!!

"And were you guys there when Pappy was chasing the dogs chasing the chickens and shouting at Oke not to break the fence down?!"

"Ha! And then Oke kicked it down anyway!"

"But not the second time! He knew better!"

Artie, tears in his eyes, gasped for air.

"Oh, that donkey wanted to, didn't he?!"

"He sure did!"

Today had been, as old Chuck would say, one for the ages.

"Hey!" Kimmie all of a sudden exclaimed. "Who is that walking around in the house?"

Everyone looked to the kitchen window.

"Who is that? That's not Kitty Cat, is it?"

"No. That's not Kitty."

"Well, it sure isn't Buddy."

"Come on," Artie said. "Let's go take a look-see."

A minute later, the night owls were gathered on the porch rail, looking in.

"Why, that's Elwood. What's Elwood doing in there?"

They all stared a minute.

Then Peto said, "I think he's eating a cookie."

"Yeah. He's eating a cookie."

"I'm goin' in," Artie said. He scampered over, hopped onto the window sill, and peered in. "It's a cookie, all right. He's got a whole jar of 'em! And, oh, my gosh! He's got a whole spread set out! It's like the Last Supper or some medieval banquet or something in there!"

Others joined Artie on the windowsill.

"Hey, look at this," Chloe said. "I think the window's not shut all the way. Oh, it's not! I can almost fit my head in here!"

Everyone else tried.

"It smells good in there, doesn't it?"

"Sure does."

"Is that the lingering aroma of cornbread I smell?"

They took a big, all together sniff!

Ahhhh!

Artie tested the window.

"Hey, give me a hand here."

Everyone joined him.

"All right, all right," he said. "All at once. On three."

"One, two, and three!" Everyone lifted. The window moved!

"One more time!"

A minute later, Artie was in, and once Artie was in, everyone was. Even Gordo fit his big butt through the narrow gap.

*   *   *

Oh, great.

Elwood didn't notice them until it was too late. If he had, he might have tried to shut the window first. As it was, the night was pretty much in tatters.

Word spreads quickly among squirrels, evidently.

It wasn't long after that they were swarming in that blasted crack in the window. Some had come all the way from over in the orange grove.

"Hey," one of them said. "What's that you're eating? Can I have a bite?"

"Uh, no. You can't."

What plebes! What novices!

"Oh, my gosh! I love these things! What are they called?!"

Elwood rolled his eyes.

"They're called cashews, and would you please finish one before you start on a second one? Pap is not made of money, you know."

It was like they had no home training at all. Elwood had to constantly school them: "Hey, do you have to leave a trail of crumbs behind you?" And, "There's a dishrag right over there, you know." And, "That's a chandelier, pal, not a swing."

Not to mention the conversation was less than electrifying.

"Don't worry about Grampy Chuck. He's sound asleep. He wears earplugs because Grammy snores."

Elwood was wishing he had his own earplugs. That was until he heard the big news of the day.

"What?! A battle?!"

"Epic, dude!"

"And they sent Vic running?!"

"Oh, you should'a seen it! With his stump between his legs! Ha!"

"And Grandma was in on it, too?!"

"Are you kiddin', dude?! She was, like, the ultimate hero! Runnin' total interference, dude! Like, you should'a seen her go!"

Elwood couldn't get enough. In fact, he broke out Grandma's bottle of cooking sherry.

"Drinks on me!"

From there, the party only got better.

Yaaa-hooooo!!

*   *   *

Pappy yawned and scratched his head. He was headed downstairs for a midnight snack. He produced another cavernous yawn as he opened the kitchen door. His mouth froze in mid-gape.

His eyes, three times their normal size, told him he had just walked in on a squirrel party. Squirrels were everywhere, on the table and the countertops. One was even hanging from the chandelier.

Instantly, they all froze, staring back at him.

And is that a ... possum in the butter dish?

Pappy's sleepy eyes narrowed. They darted back and forth, taking in the sight.

Slowly, he backed out, letting the door swing closed behind him.

He started to say something to himself, come up with some explanation, but then he shook his head, turned, and headed back upstairs.

He crawled back in bed, gently shook Grandma, and mumbled, "There's a thousand squirrels in your kitchen." He paused, reflecting, and added, "I suppose they'll leave when they're done."

"Mm-hm," Grandma replied, sleepily. "That's nice."

*   *   *

A few minutes later, Grandma's eyes opened.

She looked around. There was Pap, snoozing peacefully.

"Did I hear that? Or was I dreaming?"

She got up, put her slippers on, and headed downstairs. She peeked in the kitchen door.

It appeared to be true. There were a thousand squirrels in her kitchen.

It was indeed a squirrel party.

Grandma gaped a moment more. Then she closed the door and turned her back to it. Her face was ashen. She stood there a good long while.

Finally, she mumbled, "Pap's right. They'll probably leave when they're done. It's probably just a horrible nightmare anyway."

With that, she turned and headed back up the stairs, back to bed.

The next morning, Grandma got up as usual.

She imagined she'd had a crazy dream that there had been a squirrel party in her kitchen. It had seemed so real that she was fearful of opening the kitchen door.

Hesitantly, she did.

"Hm. I guess it was a dream after all. It had to be a dream. I mean, a possum in the butter dish?"

It was actually cleaner than usual, she thought. There were no crumbs on the table from Pap's midnight snack.

She noticed the window. It was cracked more than she normally left it for her little gecko friend. Then there was the out-of-place dishrag.

"Who left that there?" she wondered aloud.

*   *   *

Just around the corner, Elwood was breathing hard.

"Darn it! I forgot the dishrag!"

He'd barely had everyone out when he heard Grandma's alarm go off upstairs. But he'd done it.

"Hoo!"

He watched Grandma a while, going about her business, getting breakfast started. He sighed. Then he retired up to bed, to his Vacuum Cleaner Bag box.

A few minutes later, Elwood was sound asleep.

*   *   *

Buddy and Pap were having their breakfast.

Buddy wondered why the kitchen smelled like squirrels. It was bad enough that it had reeked of possum for the last week for some reason. That wasn't important, though. The important thing at the moment was filling the void in his belly.

Yummy! He wagged his tail joyfully. *This is good! Thanks, Grandma! You're the best!*

"You're kidding," Pappy was saying to Grandma. "I dreamed the same thing! It was like a squirrel party in here."

"I know!" Grandma exclaimed. "And a possum! In my dream, there was a possum in the butter dish!"

Pappy's brow did a somersault.

"You saw the possum, too?"

"Uh … … you, too?"

The two old folks looked at each other.

Then Pap said, "I reckon it's best we don't tell anyone, Zippie-doo. We're gettin' along in years, ya know. We start tellin' stories like that and before ya know it, they'll be callin' the men in the white coats to haul us off to Chattahoochee."

"Oh, they will not," Grandma said dismissively. "But it is weird, isn't it?"

Buddy thought it was weird, too.

Later on, Pap was going on about the armadillo – again.

"That does it," he grumbled as he gobbled down his Cheerios. "I'm gonna do like Cousin Terry says and toss mothballs around the house and drive that pestilence away, never to return! We'll all just have to get used to smelling like mothballs."

"But," Grandma replied, "won't he, or she, be homeless?"

Pap and Buddy looked at each other. Mutual understanding passed between them.

Buddy had told Pap how Harlan – a boy's name by the way, Buddy had asked – had assisted in rescuing Kitty, but Pap did not want to hear it. Fact was, Buddy was softening towards Harlan. He seemed like a real nice sort of fellow, putting aside the possibility of leprosy and/or cooties.

Pap grabbed his sticks of bacon, put all but one in his pocket, broke off a piece and handed it to Buddy.

"Come on, Buddy."

They were just heading out when that old, familiar pitter-patter could be heard coming down the stairs.

"Hey, Pappy!" Annie exclaimed. "Are you ready for the big calling contest today?!"

Buddy sighed. He was *not* interested in a calling contest. He looked to Pap, hoping he felt the same way.

Grandma's eyes went to Annie, then to Pap, who mumbled, "Right. The calling contest." He pursed his lips. Then he waved his hand, and said, "I'll be home at the regular time." Then, "Come on, Buddy."

Buddy looked at Annie and at Grandma. He sighed. Then he followed Pap out the door.

Later on, he was under his porch. He had not yet filled in the connector hole between his under-the-porch and Harlan's under-the-porch.

"You know," Harlan was saying, "humans can carry leprosy, too. And dogs as well, I might add."

"Really?" Buddy said. "Well ... what about cooties?"

"It is true," Harlan sighed. "Armadillos can have cooties, but I've uh ... I've been tested."

"Really?"

"Oh, absolutely."

"That's good to hear," Buddy said. "That's mighty good to hear."

Chapter Sixteen

Marv was singing his heart out. He had been up half the night at the piano, composing the soon to be award-winning *Ballad of Buddy and the Dirty Rotten Scoundrels from Next Door*. An alternative title was *The Ballad of the Battle of Icky Springs*.

Marv was still deciding.

The work was symphonic in both scale and scope, with harrowing highs and transitory, enigmatic lows.

Marv was belting it out like there was no tomorrow. He was considering making it into an opera.

On top of the telephone pole, on top of the world. It is an old saying among mockingbirds.

There was a commotion in the yard. Marv flew down to perch on the gardenia bush for a listen-in.

A calling contest, huh?

All the kids were there, plus several adults.

Uncle Amos had come earlier to set up his cameras.

"Don't you kids mess with these!"

Marv had heard Pap saying Uncle Amos was "persnickety" with his camera equipment.

Marv returned to his spot on top of the telephone pole.

Bets around the farm and the surrounding acres were running three to one in favor of Grandma. Everyone knew it was Grandma that fed Buddy – enough said.

Not to mention Pap could be cranky.

Yet everyone had seen how Buddy was with Pap. He followed him everywhere. Back when Pap was putting in the foundation for the new packing shed and running the compactor round and round packing down the dirt, Buddy had stuck right with him the whole time. All day long, hour upon hour, there went Pap and his compactor, followed close at heel by his loyal, royal hound.

Yep. It was a tough call: Grandma or Pap? Pap or Grandma?

They were all waiting on Pap. He would be home soon.

Marv kept a look out, up the grassy lane.

He turned back towards the yard, and snapped, "Darn it, son! Do you have to sneak up on me like that?!"

Junior shrugged. "Calling contest, huh?"

"That's what I hear," Marv replied.

"Well," Junior said, "I put all my money on Grandma."

Marv looked askance at his son. "But ... you don't have any money."

"Sure, I do. Mom gave me some for cleaning up my room."

Marv stared. He wanted to shout, "That's *my* money you're betting! And you shouldn't be getting paid for cleaning your own room!!"

Instead, he mumbled, "And you bet it all on a calling contest?"

"Sure did," Junior stated with pride. "I've learned how to game the system."

Marv rolled his eyes.

"So, Pop," Junior said. "Mom said it would be okay if I add onto my room. I need a place to put my new workout machine. Betty and Veronica said I have nice pecs."

Marv sighed; real heavy-like. There were many things he wanted to say.

Instead, he burst out in song, spouting forth a glorious, harrowing-height, full rendition of *The Ballad of the Battle of Icky Springs*.

"Hey, Pop. So, hey, Pop! So, can I start on the new addition?"

Marv ignored him. It was his only advantage, the God-blessed ability to ignore.

*   *   *

This was it.

Buddy was not happy about it. Or excited. Or anything but dreadful.

He was hanging with the kids out on the front porch, waiting for Pap's truck to rattle up the driveway.

Everyone was surprised to see Grandma come outside and walk around the corner of the porch without a word. She passed the bird feeder, then proceeded to the front yard.

"What's that in her hand?" someone asked.

"Looks like some kind of canister."

Everyone watched intently, Buddy as well.

Several hands were petting him simultaneously – good positioning on Buddy's part.

When she got near the oak tree, Grandma sat down on the ground, pulled a tiny white flag from her apron, stuck it in the ground, and opened up a canister. She started eating, and looking up into the tree.

"Want some?" she asked, holding them out conciliatorily. "They're cashews! My favorite!"

*   *   *

"Yo, Artie!" Halsey shouted. "Your girlfriend's out there, dude!"

Artie put his remote down and came outside.

"Look, Artie," Patsy said. "White flag. I think she's surrendering."

"Or perhaps a better way of looking at it," a wizened voice spoke from the balcony above, "is that it is simply a plea for peace. Perhaps it is not a flag of surrender, but one of truce. And hope. A request for a new beginning. A request that we should respect."

"Ha!" Peto laughed. "And it has nothing to do with last night?!"

Chloe elbowed Peto, scolding him with her eyes.

"Oh," Peto said, realizing Chuck had no idea about the shindig in the kitchen last night. "Uh, I mean … uh, maybe it *is* a flag of truce. That's right! Yes! Truce and hope are good … right?"

Everyone looked to Artie.

"Yes," Artie said, looking up at Chuck. "Truce and hope are good."

"And," he said, "those nuts in Grandma's hand look mighty good as well, don't they?"

Everyone mumbled agreements.

Artie looked up at Chuck, and the old squirrel said, "Blessed are the peacemakers, for they shall be called the Children of God."

"Yes," Artie repeated. "Blessed are the peacemakers."

With that, he looked at the others, acknowledging one and all. Then he proceeded, alone, down the gnarled trunk of the aged tree.

*   *   *

"Oh, my gosh! Look! One of them is coming down! One's coming down!"

All were in a bustle.

Uncle Amos was there, and yes, the cameras were rolling.

All watched with blithesome, buoyant hearts as the squirrel approached, almost as if he had done this before. Grandma held out her hand, and the tiny fellow scampered right up to it. He looked at the nut, tilted his head this way, and that, then took it from her hand.

He ran a few feet away and munched on it.

When he finished, he approached Grandma again.

"Oh, my gosh! I think she's crying!"

This, of course, prompted other observers to follow suit.

"Oh, how touching!"

Grandma extended gracious, welcoming hands. To everyone's surprise, the squirrel hopped right onto her lap.

"OH, MY GOSH!"

There it sat, looking at Grandma. Gently, she reached out to touch it. Tentatively, she petted it.

Tears of joy flowed from all hearts, and everyone knew the Squirrel Wars were finally over. Yes, peace and harmony would reign across this blessed land forever and ever more.

The tender moment was abruptly interrupted by the clunky emanations of an old, cranky, red pickup truck, heading up the grassy lane.

Rattle! Rattle! Honk! Honk!

Pappy waved; and as if a switch had been thrown, the kids, and Buddy, dashed out to greet the old man, who was driving real, real slow so they could all pile in the back.

"Hey, Mammy!" Pap shouted as he passed Grandma, sitting under the tree and looking all sad. He stopped the truck. "What's wrong, Mammy?" He paused. "You didn't ... you didn't find the ... body, did you?"

Grandma shook her head and waved him on so the kids, and Buddy, could have their traditional one hundred foot ride down the grassy lane to the garage.

*   *   *

The kids, and Buddy, swarmed Pappy as they made their way over from the garage, a building the big, red truck never had seen the inside of.

The adults, still gathered on the side porches, could hear Pap and the kids talking excitedly about the upcoming calling contest. Pap seemed engaged, possibly gloating already as well.

"Really, Pappy?!" one of his adoring fans asked. "You have a secret weapon?!"

"Ohhh," Pap replied. "Pap's toolbox is full of secret weapons! Right, Buddy?!"

"Woof!"

"But," little Timmy asked, "how come none of your secret weapons have worked to catch the armadillo?"

Pappy's brow indicated deep thought, and he said, "I have not yet deployed my secret weapons in that regard, sir."

The children looked on with admiration and starstruck wonder.

The adults gathered on the porch looked on with snickers and snide comments.

Grandma was there, waiting with the others, still wiping tears of joy and redemption from her eyes.

"Hey, Maw!" Pap shouted as he and entourage rounded the end of the porch.

"Yes, sweetheart?"

"I hope you can handle a sound defeat, ma'am," he said in his horrid John Wayne voice. "This ain't gonna be a walk in the park, like fightin' off a pack of wild, deranged dogs, ya know!"

Chuckles emanated from all directions. Grandma, however, remained unmoved.

"We shall see," she responded in her cool, confident, Queen Elizabeth voice.

Davy asked, "You want me to get you your frosty Big Red now, Grandfather?"

All sounds ceased – even from the observers in the trees and perched along the telephone lines.

All looked to Pappy, who swelled with pride, and to Davy, who said, "Pap thinks it's a good idea that we should call him Grandfather from now on."

"And," Pap interjected, "call Grandma Grandmother. We are civilized around here, you know."

He smiled at Grandma. She rolled her eyes.

It was a hit with the kids, though, and they all started calling him Grandfather, and he in turn called them Granddaughter or Grandson.

"Why, yes, Granddaughter Connie. It's nice to see you again as well."

They were all out there a good long while, saying howdy-dos, making greetings and salutations – and passing a few secret handshakes.

The adults, meanwhile, waited.

"Hey!" Uncle Amos said, from behind one of his synchronized cameras, "I think we should call you something more lyrical, more poetic, like … Crappy Pappy!"

Everyone laughed.

Ha-ha-ha-ha-ha!

"Hmph," Pappy retorted, defending his ground. "I'd think Snappy or *Happy* Pappy would be more fitting, don't you?"

That one got the biggest laughs of all, actually.

HAAA-HA-HA-HA-HA-HA!!!

Pap took a long swig from his ice cold, Big Red soda, which made his face scrunch up delightedly.

He scowled, unconvincingly, and mumbled, "Fine. Grandfather Crappy Pappy it shall be."

The kids cheered and fawned all over the crotchety old geezer.

"All right, all right," Pap said, tilting his straw hat back on his head. "I suppose we should get this done. So, how do we do it?"

No one seemed to know, except for Annie, who started giving directions. She had obviously seen it in her imagination, which begged the question: Did Annie know how this battle to end all battles would end?

Chapter Seventeen

Buddy wondered how Annie knew so much about calling contests. He assumed it was because she was a five year old girl, and five year old girls know all about these sort of things.

Regardless, she had them stand twenty paces apart, right there in the side yard, between the house and the turnout. Annie had assumed the role of Moderator. She had at first called it "The person in the middle with Buddy," but Pap had told her that would make her the Moderator.

Just as things were about to start, Buddy sidled over to Pap.

Um, look, he said, *I think I should mention that you have bacon in your pocket.*

"Huh?"

Pap looked in his pocket, and sure enough, there was a whole stick of bacon in there.

Without hesitation, Pap announced, "Listen up, everyone! Something has come to our attention. It was not preplanned, I assure you."

He held up the evidence so all could see.

"It turns out I have a piece of bacon in my pocket. From this morning."

A gasp arose from the crowd.

Was that his secret weapon?!

Deception?! Treachery?!!

Diabolical!!!

Buddy was horrified by the stain this could put on Pap, to be known as a potential cheater. Worse yet, he had been turned in, exposed, by Buddy himself: the squealer, the rat, the Benedict Arnold!

"Again," Pap affirmed, "I had no knowledge of this bacon in my pocket, other than the fact that I stuck it there this morning. Believe me, I would have eaten it long ago if I remembered it was there."

Thank goodness, Grandma came to the rescue, and declared, to Buddy's relief, "It is true, one and all! Pap would never be able to not eat that piece of bacon over a whole, entire day if he remembered it was there!"

Pap stood taller, his eyes meshing with those of Grandma.

"Now, there!" he announced to all. "That would be only one reason that I married that woman!"

"Stop calling her 'that woman'!" Aunt Charlotte shouted from the gallery.

"Pardon," Pappy corrected. "I meant that *darned good* woman! And," he added, "not only because that darned good woman deflected any suspicion of wrongdoing from me, but because she voluntarily, daily, chooses to admit her love for such a scurrilous fiend as I!"

A mix of cheers, jeers, and various jocular declamations filled the air.

Pap looked at Buddy. "I'm sorry, Buddy." Then he said to everyone else, "Forgive me, my people."

With that, he held up the strip of bacon, inspected it, brushed something off it, and gobbled it down.

"Mmmm. That ... is mighty gooood."

The response was mostly jeers this time, some hisses and boos, and a wide sampling of yucks and ews.

Pappy looked at Annie, and said, "Back to you, kiddo ... I mean, back to you, Granddaughter Moderator Annie!"

A minute later, Annie had Buddy in starting position, right in the middle of the two contestants. He was sitting, like a good boy.

Buddy was not happy, however. In fact, this was the worst thing ever to happen to him. He did not want to offend either one. He loved both of them, and for different reasons. His only option was to figure out who would take it the least hard; then he would go to the other one.

Still, he could see it in their eyes. Either would be crushed if he chose the other.

Everyone was watching.

*   *   *

Never had there been such a contentious moment at The Last Resort; not since the day before, anyway.

All bets were in and final. Everyone was waiting on Uncle Amos.

"I thought you said everything was ready to roll," Pap griped.

Uncle Amos glared at his brother.

"It's this stupid camera, dude! The stupid, dynamic integrated parallax sensitivity filters keep goin' haywire!"

Marv observed from his post on the pole. A true bird's eye view.

Grandma was positioned at the hot bathtub end of the yard. Pappy was at the grassy lane end. In the middle was the Moderator, bursting with excitement and squirming in her little kids' seat so much that it appeared she was in danger of falling out of it.

Next to her was Buddy, the subject of the experiment.

Marv thought Buddy looked forlorn – or possibly suicidal.

"Got it!" Uncle Amos shouted. "Ready to roll!"

110

Finally!

A second later. "Action!"

All eyes went to the Moderator, who appeared suddenly nervous and unsure what to do.

"Go ahead, sweetie," Grandma said.

Annie seemed to recover.

She rested her hand on Buddy, and said, "On your marks! Get set!" She paused, all eyes on her. "GO!"

"Here, Buddy," Grandma said.

"Come on, Buddy," Pappy said.

Buddy didn't move. He looked to the one, then the other, but he sat right on his haunches and did not move.

The action picked up.

"Come on, Buddy!" Pap said louder.

"Here, Buddy!" Grandma said louder.

Yep. Action-packed.

Annie prodded Buddy. "Go on, Buddy. It's okay. Pick one."

But Buddy would not pick.

Riveting.

"Hey, Pop."

"Darn it!" Marv said. "How many times I gotta tell you not to sneak up on me?"

"Oh, sorry, Pop, but Betty says she likes hair gel on guys. Do you think I could borrow a few bucks? Till later?"

Marv looked at Junior, annoyed. "Um, I'm kind of busy right now, son. And what do you mean, borrow? You plan on getting a job soon? To pay it back?"

"Oh. Oh, yeah. Sure, Pop. I'm working on that, but for right now, I just need a few bucks to hold me over. Mom said it was no problem."

Marv tried to pay attention to the thrilling, death-defying contest below.

"Come on, Buddy!" Pap shouted even louder than the last time.

"Here, Buddy!" Grandma shouted as well.

"But," Marv asked his son. "Don't you have money riding on this, Junior?"

"Oh, sure thing, Pop. Easy money."

Marv sighed. He returned his attention to the contestants, both of whom had progressed from chirpy biddings to shameless groveling.

"Please, Buddy? ... Please?"

And, "Please, Buddy? ... Please?"

It appeared it would be a stalemate, but then Buddy got to his feet.

The crowd gasped in anticipation, but then Buddy sat back down. He scratched behind his ear.

By now, Pappy had changed tactics.

"BUDDY! COME!! BAD DOG!"

Grandma had changed her tactics as well, except she had a different ploy.

She stooped, held her hand out, and said, "Come on, little Choopie-poo."

Everyone looked at one another, and all mumbled in unison, "Choopie-poo?"

Apparently, Grandma had a secret weapon: Choopie-poo.

Buddy got up again. He lowered his head and leaned in the direction of Grandma.

Pap, meanwhile, was in a dither. An uproar!

"NO! NO, BUDDY! Look at me! It's me! Your benevolent leader! Your best pal! I love you, Buddy! I love you!"

Buddy halted. He looked back. Desperation oozed from Pappy's eyes.

But then, from the other direction, came a soft, tantalizing voice: "Come on, Choopie-poo." Then Grandma pulled out the big guns. Yep. She went into full-throttle, baby-talk mode. "Come on wittle Choopie-woopie. Come see your Mommy-wommy."

Again, Buddy hesitated.

Pappy, sensing a turn in the tide, pulled the old turnabout. Yes, he switched to baby-talk, too, which he wasn't that good at.

"Come on, little Poopy-loopy."

"Poopy-loopy?!" someone shouted from the gallery, and everyone laughed. Not only that, it appeared Buddy wasn't really that fond of the Poopy-loopy moniker himself.

It was clear to Marv that Grandma had Pap on the ropes.

"Come on, wittle Choopie-woopie."

The Choopie-woopie weapon seemed invincible. Indomitable.

"Come on, Buddy," the old codger begged. "Please?!" he pleaded. "Pretty please with sugar on top! Please!!"

And there it was.

Pity.

Yes, there was pity in Buddy's eyes. Pity for Pap. He took a step towards him.

But Grandma returned fire with all guns. That's right: she used super-duper, way over the top, baby talk: "Come on wittle Choopie-woopie-woopie-woo!"

Pappy was relentless, however. He sniffed; then he wiped at his eye, as if he might be crying. But he did not stop there. Oh, what a dirty fighter Pap was. He stooped as low as stoop can go. That's right. He pulled out the oldest trick in the book. That's right. The old guilt trip.

"Buddy! You can't do this to me, Buddy! After all we've been through together. After all I've done for you! You can't do this to me! Your old pal! Your greatest pal of pals!!"

Marv, meanwhile, was ignoring Junior, who was going crazy, shouting for Grandma to go for the guilt trip as well. And the pity party, too!

But, evidently Grandma, unlike Pap, had standards.

It looked like the contest was going one way, and one way alone.

Pap was pathetic.

Then, out of the corner of his eye, Marv noticed something out by the orange grove. Marv understood Buddy's predicament, even if no one else did. Buddy needed help out there. And here? Here was opportunity.

Marv flitted away.

"Hey, Pop! Where you going?"

Marv ignored Junior. He had a job to do. He was, after all, the official watchbird around here.

When he got to the gardenia bush, he got Buddy's attention.

"Hey!" he pointed. "Look over there!"

Buddy looked, and that was that, for there was nothing more tantalizing, more appealing, more fun than one thing, and that thing started with the word Chasing and ended with the word Rabbits. So there went Buddy, dashing right past Pap – *Whoosh!* – across the grassy lane and into the orange grove.

Gone.

"BUDDY!" Pap shouted. "HEY! BUDDY! ... BAD DOG!!" But there was no sign of Buddy.

Pappy turned to the gathered, a helpless expression on his face; then he threw up his arms and mumbled, "Fine," and he turned and shouted, "Go get 'em, Buddy! Good dog!!"

As would be expected, all were shocked, aghast at the outcome of the calling contest.

Yes. The rabbit won.

Marv flew back up to his telephone pole. It felt good, doing something helpful.

"Hey, Pop. Can I get that loan now?"

Marv ignored Junior, though, and all those other bothersome things in life. Instead, he listened to the sounds of a happy dog, somewhere out in that orange grove, running his big heart out, and enjoying being nothing more than who he was.

"Woof!"

Epilogue

Hot bathtub time.

Buddy and Pap were relaxing. No one did it better.

You know, Buddy said. *I been thinking.*

"Oh? What you been thinkin' about, old pal of pals?"

Well, Buddy said, his handsome, philosophical brow furrowing. *I think I prefer 'Pappy' over 'Grandfather'.* He paused. *You know?*

"Really," Pap said. "I kind of like 'Grandfather,' myself. It sounds so ... so formal, don't you think?"

Well, yes, it does, old pal of pals. But I think that's what seems so out of place. I don't know if you know it, Pap, Buddy said, trying to be gentle, *but, well, we're just not the real formal types. By us, I mean all the Loxleys. We're more, say ... earthy – in a good way, of course. We're the unpretentious kind, more plain and humble, folksy kind of folks. You know?*

I mean look at me. I'm a mutt ... kind of like you, don't you think? We should be proud of who we are, Pap. Why, I've heard you say those very same words before ... you know?

Pap seemed deep in thought. He took up his pipe and had a puff.

After a while, he nodded.

"You know, Buddy," he said, "I'm glad I have you."

Well, I'm glad I have you, too, Pap. So, Buddy ventured. *No hard feelings about the calling contest?*

"Are you kiddin'? There's nothing could ever come between us. And just between you and me, I expected you to go for Grandma the whole time."

Really?

"Oh, yes. I bet on it, in fact, that you'd go to her. I mean," Pappy pursed his lips. "I gotta tell you, I'd'a probably gone for Grandma myself if the contest was between you and her. But I gotta say, I am impressed that you gave me such a fighting chance. I mean, between Grandma and me? She's a much better choice, by any standard."

Buddy nodded. *I'll remember that for the next time.*

"I don't blame you if you do, Buddy," Pappy said. He looked askance at his pal. "So ... Choopie-poo, huh?"

Buddy shrugged. *Laugh if you want. I kind of like it.*

*   *   *

Grandma was doing a little cleaning, a little vacuuming. She never stopped doing a bit here, a bit there.

She was humming a happy tune, rummaging around in the broom closet. She worked her way to the back and reached up into the box labeled "Vacuum Cleaner Bags."

*   *   *

Pap and Buddy were relaxing. No one did it better.

From the direction of the house, they heard an abrupt and sudden "AAAAAAAAAH!!!"

"Oo," Pappy said. "That can't be good."

Mm, Buddy replied. *I don't suppose so.*

… And neither do we.

The End

Find more of Tim Robinson's books at atroicalfrontier.com or amazon.com/author/timrobinson.